BEYOND SCARS

A GRIPPING TALE OF LOVE, LOSS AND RESILIENCE.

ALKA DIMRI SAKLANI

Copyright © Alka Dimri Saklani
All Rights Reserved.

Contents

Contents

Contents

Part 1

CHAPTER ONE

VIVAAN

Sometimes, when people touch our scars, they touch our soul.

It was going to be a big day, though I didn't know it at the time. It was my first art exhibition. Was I nervous? Maybe. It was difficult for me to accept that because, for a very long time in my life, I trained myself not to feel any emotion. But then I looked at my paintings and laughed at myself. What a liar I had been!

I watched the large colorful paintings hanging on the white wall, each one illuminated by the track lighting above it. The light background music added to the ambiance of the event.

It was 6.00 PM but no one was here yet. Was I too hopeful? Before I could doubt myself again, I saw some people entering my studio-cum-art gallery. Arjun, my friend, welcomed them all. I had already mentioned that I didn't want to be introduced as the artist, so I silently watched the people judging my art.

"Wow, this painting is nice, it's perfect for our library." A middle-aged woman said to her partner, referring to a painting of a pile of books. I was glad she liked the painting but what she said next disappointed me. "It will match our peach walls."

She wanted it only because it matched her walls? What about the message the art portrayed? Or maybe she failed to see it.

I walked to a group of teenagers watching the painting of a butterfly.

"It's wonderful. I just loved the colour combination," a girl said to the boy standing next to her.

He nodded thoughtfully. "Just look at the details," he said, and a smile lit up my face. Maybe he could see beneath the colours. "The way every nuance melt into the other, the way each part of her wings is painted. I just love it."

My smile faded. Though I loved what he noticed, it would've been great if he looked a little deeper, beyond the shades and the strokes.

I walked to an elderly couple who were watching the painting of a child running behind a bus.

"I want this one. Doesn't he look like Ishu?" The elderly woman's voice reflected longing.

"Yeah, quite similar," her husband replied. "Yesterday he was saying, 'Grandpa when are you coming down to meet me'."

I guess they didn't look into the eyes of the kid, else they would not have made the comparison. The more I eavesdropped on different conversations, the more disappointed I became. Passing through many paintings I reached the painting of a box of toys. I wondered if anyone could see beyond the bright shades and the scattered toys in the painting. A loud bang interrupted my thoughts, and I turned back. A few feet away from me, a boy had fallen on the ground, his face flat on the floor. All eyes in the gallery turned to him.

"Get up, dude." I offered him my hand and he looked up. Oops. He...she was a girl.

"I am sorry," I said, embarrassed.

A hint of red appeared on her cheeks. Not sure if it was because of me misunderstanding her as a boy or because of the dozen pair of eyes staring at her.

"It's okay." She took my hand and got up. Her hands were rough, unlike the hands of usual girls. A giggle caught our attention, and we looked at the source, a few feet away a little girl was trying to suppress her laughter by pressing her palm on her mouth, and her mother was instructing her to behave herself.

"It's ok, it was funny. Let her laugh." She forced a smile and walked away, ignoring the scrutiny of the eyes still on her.

Wow. This girl was embarrassed but she laughed it off. A rare quality. She had all my attention now. She was a perfect tomboy of medium height, wearing blue jeans, a blue denim jacket, and sports shoes. There was a bounce in her steps.

"Hey, blunder queen!" A boy came behind her, laughing, and slapped the back of her head playfully. They resembled each other, though the boy was a few inches taller.

"Shut up, Avinash," the girl said, offended.

"Now that you've finally made a blunder, you must be feeling better," the boy teased her.

"Hey Avni, are you all right?" Arjun walked up to her. It seemed he knew her.

She nodded, and the boy mocked her, "it's only now that she must be fine."

"Come on, Avinash. Stop teasing her." Arjun said.

"How can he stop teasing me?" she said and walked towards the painting of the butterfly.

The moment this girl called Avni had laughed off her embarrassment, she had gained my attention, and I wanted to know what she thought about my paintings. She looked intently at the butterfly as if she could see beyond the brush strokes and the colours. She traced her fingers over the vibrant hues of the wings of the butterfly and a smile enveloped her face. Nobody could touch the paintings, but maybe she didn't know the rules. And somehow, I liked how her fingers admired the paintings and I didn't feel the need to stop her. Her eyes moved down the painting and her fingers slowly danced over the fallen leaves. For a fraction of a second, her smile faded as she touched the broken flower hidden beneath the pile of dried leaves. Or did I imagine it?

She slowly walked to the next painting. The painting of the books. She traced her fingers over the books and I knew she was studying the painting, not just watching it. Her finger traced down to the last book hidden in the pile. It lingered a little longer on the torn edge of the book, then traced to the few pages shattered on the floor, and my heart skipped a beat.

She suddenly looked towards me and caught me staring at her. Thankfully, she wasn't offended and gave me a warm smile.

"Soulful paintings, aren't they?" she asked.

Her words touched something deep within me. A lot of people said my paintings were beautiful, but for the first time, someone said they were soulful.

"It depends how you look at it," I replied.

"Yeah, you are right. Do you know what they say about paintings? That paintings are silent poems. And they also say that no two people read the same poem in the same way."

"That was deep." I took a step towards her. "So, what do you think about these paintings?"

"Something is common in all these paintings."

"What?"

"Something is broken."

Her words did something crazy to my heart, and I looked at her face closely. I wasn't sure if she was pretty, but something in her face was captivating. Maybe her eyes that were a deep dark brown. Eyes that could see beyond the outer layer. Before I could say anything, she further surprised me.

"And the thing that is broken is almost hidden."

Impossible! How did she comprehend it? And did I say I loved her husky voice?

She moved to the next painting—that of the boy running behind the bus, and I followed her as if in a trance.

She traced her finger over the face of the boy. "See? It's not just a bus he has missed. The pain in his eyes says he is running behind something, something he is afraid to lose. And look at this small heart-shaped pendant he is wearing. It's broken and almost hidden under his T-shirt."

She moved to the next painting and I followed her, almost scared. What if she missed what this piece was about?

"In the heap of these toys, look at this toy house hidden under the pile." She pointed at that house. "It's broken too."

What I felt that moment was something I hadn't felt in...I guess...forever. Sometimes you didn't want your art to be appreciated, you wanted it to be understood.

She stared at me directly for the first time and I realized that her eyes had hues of black amid the brown. Her skin was soft, unlike her hands. There wasn't a trace of make-up on her face and I liked that.

"Hey, Avni. So, what did you find in these paintings?" The boy who resembled her hopped into our conversation.

"They are awesome." She didn't give out any details. Maybe, sharing her thoughts with a stranger was easier for her. So, we had something in common. I wondered if someday we could become friends. But then, would she talk to me the way she just did with that boy?

"Have you decided if you want to purchase any of these?"

She glanced around and walked towards a painting towards the end of the room. It was a painting of a girl wearing a saree, looking in the mirror. The mirror that was broken at the edge didn't reflect her; it reflected a different woman.

"Don't be like her, Avni," the boy said, and the way he said it, I was sure he wasn't talking about the painting. The girl stepped back from the painting and the easy demeanor between them shifted to obvious tension.

"Yeah, I guess I don't want this," she said dryly, her fingers tracing the painting—the girl standing in front of the mirror, the girl in the reflection, and the broken edge of the mirror.

Which part of the painting made her sad? Which part did she connect with?

Suddenly, I wanted to paint Avni for reasons unknown. I talked with Arjun and my other friends but from the corner of my eye, I kept watching her. Sometimes she caught me doing so, but she wasn't offended. She simply gave me a friendly smile.

That night, after returning home, I just couldn't shrug off her words...broken and hidden. I needed to wake up early the next morning but somehow, I just couldn't sleep. To get some sleep tonight, I needed to put my mind at rest.

I tried to recall her face. All the while she was at the gallery, I saw her from different angles but hardly ever from the front. I mixed a few colors and my hands started moving on the canvas of their own volition. I meekly followed my intuitions and gave into the trance that was guiding me. And when I came out of my trance, my canvas had captured something new for the first time.

Nothing was broken.

Though a lot was hidden. One shade behind the other, all chaos. But beautiful chaos. It was Avni. And I knew she had touched a part of me.

CHAPTER TWO

AVNI

We were in the college canteen, sipping tea. It was my friend Shreyansh's birthday so there were more people at our table than our usual group of three.

Shreyansh got furious when his mother called. "If I could give one piece of advice to my parents it would be to stop being so nosey." He disconnected the phone and asked nobody in particular, "If you could give some advice to your parents what would it be?

"Take a divorce," I said, and all heads turned towards me.

Avinash glared at me and I just wanted to evaporate. Why couldn't I keep my mouth shut? Why did I always speak out my mind when the world worked in a diplomatic way, which meant saying things people wanted to listen to.

"Nice joke...ha ha..." I forced a smile that, I guess, failed miserably in hiding my embarrassment. I lowered my head in my cup of tea.

"Well, I would want them to be a little less romantic, especially when we are around." Avinash joked as he came to my rescue as usual. His easy tone always fooled people and the laughter that echoed around was enough proof.

Mom and dad must be the most envied couple in the town. Dad had a reputation of being a diehard romantic; the way he cared for mom at social gatherings became the reason for discontent for many women. He would bring the plate for her, check if she needed anything every few minutes. So obviously, it wasn't difficult to take my words as a bad joke. And soon enough, everyone started discussing other topics.

Avinash tapped on my head and whispered, "So ... blunder queen, today's blunder done. Mission accomplished?"

I was too embarrassed to even look at him. I lowered my head even further into the cup of tea.

"It's ok, bro," he said, and I stared hard at him.

"Oh sorry, sis," he smiled. "Though, are you my sister and not my brother?" he teased me.

We were like this all our life. Twins. Brother and sister. Though he said we were brother and brother. Two brothers. He always teased me like that.

The painting in the art gallery defined me perfectly—the girl in the mirror. Our reality gets blurred behind the masks we put on, sometimes to keep people happy and sometimes just to survive. Our mind has its way of wandering from one thing to another, completely forgetting what the first thought in the chain of thoughts was. From the art gallery, my mind wandered to the guy who had offered me his hand to get up.

His hand was rough, definitely the hand of a man who has worked hard, and I liked it. It wasn't his tall stature, his tanned skin with a well-defined jaw, or his perfect demeanor that I found attractive. It was something else entirely. How do I define that thing, the one thing that set him apart from the others? Rawness. Yes, he looked raw. I know that's a strange word to define someone, but isn't it strange that I liked someone instantly? The eyes that were embarrassed at finding out that I was a girl were intense, the kind of gaze that penetrates you. Those hypnotic eyes had followed me, especially at the way I had admired the paintings. Maybe, he also connected to the paintings the way I did.

Avinash tapped his elbow at my elbow.

"Where are you lost? Your lunch is getting cold."

"Oh yeah," I said and finished my lunch.

Everyone around was busy discussing the latest cricket match. Though there was a time I loved these discussions, of late I failed to enjoy these talks. I think I didn't belong to this group so after finishing my lunch, I walked up to Priyanka, my classmate, who sat a few tables away.

"Hey, Priyanka. This dress looks so good on you." I pointed at her lavender midi, trying to get friendly with her.

"Thanks, Avni." She looked at me in confusion, as if deciding if she could say the same for me. Or maybe it was just my assumption. I had started judging myself a lot, because all my dresses were the same—black and blue jeans with slight variations in shade, cotton t-shirts with a thin denim jacket. There were no red, pink, or yellows in my wardrobe and of late, I inculcated a fantasy for those colors. The other girls joined us soon. They talked about the latest fashion, nail polish, lipstick, high heels, and off-shoulder dresses. I tried hard but couldn't contribute to the conversation. I didn't know if it was because of my lack of interest or knowledge or both.

"Avni, come. We are leaving." Avinash called out.

"Coming," I said half-heartedly. I didn't belong here with these girls too.

Where did I belong?

As we walked towards our class, the noise from the adjacent building pulled my attention. It wasn't the noise that disturbed me, it was the memories that knocked at the sight of the heap of bricks and the smell of cement. The memory I had tried hard to escape, but the one that never left me, especially on the days when dad was home. I looked at Avinash and wondered if this renovation work reminded him of that day too, but one look at him and I knew it didn't.

Or maybe he was good at pretending.

CHAPTER THREE

VIVAAN

I was getting late for college as usual. Mom was scolding me as usual.

"Mom, I don't have the time for breakfast, I need to rush," I said, tying my shoelaces.

"How many times do I have to tell you to sleep on time? I am not going to let you leave without eating your breakfast." She shoved a piece of *dhokla* in my mouth. And even after I was done tying my shoelace, she was still making me eat as she had done all these years.

"Look at you, you have lost so much weight," she said, shoving yet another bite inside my already-full mouth. Before she could put yet another bite, I gestured for her to wait and finished the overstuffed food in my mouth.

"Mom, I have put on two kilos, thanks to you." I joked.

"Two kilos? No need to lie to me, Okay?"

"Okay mom, the machine was lying and I am also lying." I picked up my bag from the sofa and slung it on my back.

"Bhaiya, can't you eat yourself? Are you also a baby?" My four-year-old brother Kanha ran up to me with his favorite toy car in his hand.

There was a solid nineteen years of age gap between us. I knew mom wanted to make sure I wasn't having any more nightmares before she could bring a new child to the house. She was the best mom in the world.

Kanha jumped on my lap. "You are a tiny baby bhaiya," he said and giggled, putting a hand on his mouth.

"Yeah, I love being a tiny baby." I pulled his cheeks, and he freed himself, getting back to playing with his car.

I waved goodbye and left. I preferred to walk to my college as it was just two km away.

It had been more than a decade, but I still couldn't figure out why I felt the way I did. Amid all the love and care, a strange sense of emptiness surrounded me. Though there were times I felt perfectly fine like everyone else around me, sometimes I felt cut off as if everything was temporary, fragile, ready to break any moment. But why was I scared of it? Why do we seek permanent things in our temporary life? I focused my mind before I could float away from the present and the girl from the art gallery started playing on my mind.

"Avni," I said her name aloud. I liked the sound of it.

And then a voice...a name echoed around and hit me straight in the gut.

Appu...

I froze, overwhelmed with emotions I had tried to ignore all my life. Further on the road, a man was running behind his child, who probably got out of his hold.

No one was calling me. Appu was the name of a child. He was as different from me as possible.

He was seven, not twenty-three.

His skin was soft and supple, not rugged like mine.

He was three feet tall, not six.

His smile was genuine. Sincere. Bright. His eyes held hope.

He didn't lose his innocence at seven.

And more than anything, he was not handicapped.

Changing that name didn't change my identity, my past, my truth.

Yes, Appu did reflect an image of my past, but I wished he didn't have a future like mine.

CHAPTER FOUR

AVNI

We walked to the canteen, me and Avinash, and we occupied a seat at one of the center tables. I cringed internally when Shreyansh walked towards me. He was the type of guy any girl would swoon at. With his perfect physique, he could qualify for the cover image of any reputed magazine. His skin was spotless behind the slight stubble. But his broad shoulders weren't ready to take responsibility when his sister was dealing with a difficult marriage. His attractive hazel eyes seldom saw good in people, his strong hands hardly worked except exercising in a gym. But these were not the things that put me off.

He walked up to me and patted my back, "Hey buddy." Then he slid beside me, a little too close for comfort. And that's exactly what put me off.

I shifted a little farther from him. His actions might be unintentional; I was just a boy in a girl's body, why would he be interested? Nevertheless, it put me off. I shifted away from him, gulped down my tea in a haste, and got up.

"What happened? Where are you going?" Avinash inquired.

"I have some assignments to complete. I am going to the library."

"But we completed them together last night."

Damn. The side effect of having a twin who didn't understand clues.

"Yes, but my conclusion was pending. You don't know about that." I walked away, but he followed. "What happened Avni? You look upset."

"I am fine, Avinash. I just need to finish my assignment." I shrugged off his concern and walked away before he could ask anything else.

My days at college were getting tougher by the day. Neither could I tolerate Shreyansh's advances nor did I enjoy the silly chatter about make-up with the girls. I just roamed around here and there before the class started. After a long day, thankfully it was time to leave. The extra lectures had stretched for long and it was almost 7 p.m. when we reached home. After dinner, the question I had been dreading was thrown at me.

"Why are you behaving so oddly for the last few days? What's the problem?" Avinash asked, following me to my room.

"I am fine, Avinash." I began to arrange my books on the table, wanting to avoid his gaze.

"No, you are not. Don't try to fool me."

I wanted to tell him about Shreyansh, but the way he always treated me like a boy that conversation wasn't easy, so I just made an excuse, "I get bored by your cricket conversations."

"So have you inculcated a fantasy for fashion talks?" He mocked me.

I thumped the book in my hand on the table and looked at him, "No, I just don't like cricket talk anymore. Is that a problem?"

"Why are you getting so worked up."

"Why can't you just let me be." I treaded out of the door and he followed.

"Where are you going?"

"I need some space to breathe, and please don't follow me." I stormed downstairs and towards the main door when mom stopped me.

"Where are you going, Avni?"

"For a walk." I rushed out before she could ask anything else.

I wasn't sure where I wanted to go. Was there even a place where I could be myself?

A girl staring in the mirror, but the reflection was not hers.

A strong pull directed my steps and within a few minutes, I was standing in front of the deserted art gallery. The small apartment-cum-studio was surrounded by a small garden laden with the fragrance of lilies. It must be closed but there was a dim light inside. I stupidly walked up to the door and tried to peek inside through a window.

Suddenly the door opened, and a guy caught me sneaking in.

Damn, why couldn't I just disappear?

He was the same big guy who had offered me his hand to get up that day.

"What are you doing here?" his gaze narrowed at me.

"What are *you* doing here?" I asked, offended, straightening my back.

"This is my studio."

Damn. As if sneaking into an art gallery at an odd hour was not stupid enough, I had to ask the owner what he was doing at his studio!

"Oh, is that so?" My voice wavered and I straightened up, pushing my hands in my pockets. "It's just that I loved the paintings and...and wanted to have another look."

"Then come inside." He gestured with his hand for me to come in.

"Well, um, oh, actually, it's very late. I will come another day." I needed to vanish at the earliest.

"It wasn't late to sneak in though?" His voice had a hint of mischief.

I had already made a fool of myself, and now there was no use hiding. So, I walked inside his studio.

The studio was almost empty and was illuminated by a dim light. All his stellar paintings were sold.

"You paint here in your studio?" I asked.

"Depends on my mood. Sometimes I paint at home, sometimes here. I just came to drop off my latest painting."

"But I can't see any painting here."

"It won't be for sale so I have kept it in a different area."

"Where?" I said and immediately bit my tongue. He didn't want to sell it so obviously, he wanted nobody to see it. "I am sorry. It's ok if you don't want to—"

"Follow me," he interrupted my stammering and walked up to a storeroom at the end of the hall. There was hardly any space for both of us in the tiny room, along with his many paintings stacked along the wall and a few stacked on the big shelf above. Suddenly it hit me we were standing in each other's space. His gigantic frame hovered over me as he pulled out a painting from the shelf above. While I was still reeling from the exotic scent of his cologne and his proximity, he turned the photo towards me and I gasped.

It was...what do I say...it was colorful. It was deep. It was dark. It was bright. It was happy. It was sad.

It was me.

A girl was looking in the mirror just like the earlier painting, but in the earlier painting, the eyes were not mine. These were my eyes. The shade of brown with a hint of black. Of course, it had to be a coincidence. He couldn't have painted me after seeing me momentarily in just one meeting! Of course not. Or could he? Could anyone see the mess in my mind, and think it was so beautiful? Was it even possible? It could only be magic. This painting communicated to me in a way no one had ever communicated.

"Are you ok?" he asked, and only then did I realize that I was shivering.

"I guess." I took the photo from his hand and stared at it for a while, before handing it back to him.

Once we were back to the studio and seated on the couch, he asked, "That painting reflects your thoughts. Right?" The way his gaze penetrated me, bothered me. It wasn't good to be so easily readable.

"Why do you think so?" I asked, looking towards the storeroom, wanting to avoid his gaze.

"Just the way you said that my paintings had something hidden and broken."

My eyes shot back to him and we communicated something in silence. What was it? A connection? Was that even possible, since I was meeting this gentleman just for the second time in my life.

"Do you paint?" Thankfully, his question came as a rescue.

"I used to, but not anymore."

"Why?"

"Couldn't paint as well as you." I smiled.

"Show them to me someday."

Was it a hint that he wanted to see me again? Why was I suddenly soaring? I hope my face didn't reflect my stupid emotions.

"Sure. Why didn't you tell me that day that you were the artist?"

"I wanted an honest opinion."

Suddenly, a loud jingle started from nowhere. 'Chanda mama door ke...' Oh shit, it was coming from my jeans pocket. Argh! Avinash must have changed the ringtone to tease me again.

"Nice ringtone." He teased me.

"Yeah, of course," I somehow managed to say as I took the call. "Yes, mom, I know it's late. Reaching in fifteen minutes." I said and disconnected the phone.

It was record-breaking. I mean, the number of times I had made a fool of myself today. I wasn't sure I could face this gentleman again when I got up to leave.

"So, when do I get to see your paintings?" he surprised me. Did he want to see me again? Of course, where else would he get so much free entertainment!

"Tomorrow? Same time same place?" I replied so quickly that I was sure I sounded desperate. I just hoped I didn't look as embarrassed as I felt.

"Sure. Then keep your promise, Avni."

"You know my name?"

"Yes, that day your friend called you Avni."

"And you are Vivaan." I knew of course. He was the painter whose art gallery I was sneaking into and now was sitting in, without even introducing myself. Of course, that was me.

CHAPTER FIVE

VIVAAN

I watched Avni as she walked away. I didn't remember the last time I smiled so much. No pretense, nothing fake and that made her rare. And yes, funny too.

Was it just a coincidence that she was here and saw her painting? Did she realize it was her painting? Different emotions had clouded her face and she was trembling. Or was she confused? Maybe someday I would tell her that I painted her. Maybe not.

After closing my studio, I walked up to Arjun's place. He was my childhood friend. He never took a leave unless his dad was in extremely bad shape, and today he was on leave.

As soon as he opened the door, I knew he needed some rest more than anything. He was the kind of person who could smile most days. But today didn't seem like most days. His complexion had turned a shade darker and his shoulders were hunched, as if his 5'10'' height had shrunk to 5'8''. Working night shifts in a call center along with his studies was taking a toll on him. His dad, his only family, had been diagnosed with cancer. Though it was the first stage, all his retirement funds had been wiped out due to his treatment.

Arjun's dad was sleeping on the living room sofa. Some utensils were scattered on the side table and the television was on. I guess he just slept while watching television. The disease had changed him drastically; his body was now just a bundle of bones and there were dark sockets under his eyes.

Arjun and I walked up to the balcony. The calm weather outside was a stark contrast to the air in his house, and we stood in silence. I was never good with words, but he just needed me by his side and not my words.

"The money is dwindling like anything…I don't know…I just don't know how I will manage…" His voice cracked as he gripped the railing and hunched a little more if that was even possible.

"Don't worry. We will work something out." I put my hand on his shoulder. "I just need a few more paintings. My next exhibition will be up in three weeks. When is the date for the next chemo?"

"The 15th of next month."

"Don't worry, we have time." My last exhibition had yielded unexpected results and I had higher hopes from the next one. I made a mental note to push myself harder. "Why don't you apply for a personal loan?" I asked him.

"Oh yeah, why didn't I think of that?" A small ray of hope shone in his eyes and we again stood in silence. It was never like this. I was always the silent one and he always had a lot to say. Nevertheless, whether we were silent or talking, we found comfort in each other's company.

After spending some time with him, I walked home. It was quiet when I entered. It meant Kanha was already asleep and dad was not home yet.

"Mom, why do you never lock the door?" I asked, stepping in. Mom was working on her laptop, sitting on the couch.

"Why do you worry so much? Our neighborhood is safe," she said, looking up from her laptop.

"But still, what's the harm in locking it?" This was the only thing for which I always argued with her.

"Ok, ok. I will lock it now onwards," she said as usual, and I knew she had just avoided the argument.

"Dad is late again?" I sat next to her.

"Yeah," she sighed. "Today he's going to get a good whipping," she said in mock anger.

"I would love to witness it." I laughed.

"What conspiracy is being planned against me?" Dad walked in with his huge smile. His smile was enough to make a tough day easy.

"Even you didn't lock the door." Mom shot a glance at me.

"Oops! Sorry." I held my ears with both hands.

Dad kept his bag on the sofa and mom shot a warning glare at him.

"Okay, Okay, I will keep it in its right place. Let me get fresh first." He said in his defense. We all knew that he would forget it after he freshened up. Finally, mom would have to keep the bag as well as his other things like his wallet, watch, mobile, etc.

"I know what you are going to do after freshening up." She shut down her laptop and picked up his things. "Kanha kept asking for you. He eventually slept. How long will this project go on?"

"Just a few weeks. Then I will be at your service, madam." He bowed in front of mom, one hand on his chest.

"My service. Huh!" Mom was not going to be charmed by him easily. I was enjoying this.

"Why? Am I not at your service always?" He got straight and hugged mom.

"You have a grown-up boy now. At least have some decency," she said, but couldn't stop the smile from lighting up her face.

"My son is grown up. He will also learn something. What say, Vivaan?" He winked at me and mom elbowed him in his waist. Then he hugged me by my shoulder and asked, "What happened? You look upset." Just one look at me and he knew it as always. I could hide my feelings from everyone but not from him and mom. If not dad, mom would have asked the question in a few minutes.

"I met Arjun today."

"How's his dad?"

"Not well. Working full time along with studies is taking a toll on Arjun."

"Vivaan, if you need any..."

"No dad, that's not what I mean." I straightened up and shook my head. An unsaid hurt marred his face. I shouldn't have been so quick to reply. "Sorry dad, but I will let you know if I need..."

"Vivaan," mom interrupted, but dad gestured her to stop. It was awful, letting them down. But, I wasn't comfortable asking for money. I didn't like it when they spent too much on me. It made me uncomfortable. I knew it frustrated mom. Dad was cool with it. Dad was cool with almost anything. I told them I needed to freshen up too and left the room.

Mom tried to keep her voice low, but I could still hear her.

"Why did you stop me, Noel? Why can't we help? We are his parents after all. Why does he need to spend sleepless nights painting to put up the exhibition and help? He doesn't need to work nonstop. It might affect his studies and his health."

"Nidhi, it will make him independent and strong."

I loved the confidence in dad's tone.

"Strong? Are you kidding me? Does he need to get any stronger? After all that has happened?" Mom's voice faltered, and I knew dad must have hugged her.

"Then maybe, he is already strong enough to take care of his issues." I found a hint of sadness in his voice. He was not sad that I was strong, he was sad at the reasons that had made me strong.

Dad was right. I was stronger now, but it was because of them. The last decade just flashed by in front of my eyes; the way they had rebuilt me from ashes. Recently, dad gave me his old office to use as my studio and he had renovated the whole place without my knowledge. What more could I ask for?

I struggled with my assignments that were supposed to be submitted two days earlier. Finally, after finishing the assignment at 2 a.m. I pulled out my mobile to set an alarm for 5 o'clock. I could paint in the morning too.

My mind was tired and so was my body and though my mind wanted to torture me a little more, my body finally shut down into a deep sleep. I failed to get up at five the next morning and cursed myself the whole day. It was a tiring day and the extra lectures stretched a little further.

There was one unread message in my inbox when I reached home at six in the evening.

"She was on our radar but now she has again left the place. We don't know where she is now. Will contact you as soon as we have some information."

I read the message again and again as if it would change the text. I didn't even try to work on my pending assignments, as I knew I couldn't focus until I put my mind to rest. I pulled up my paints and a canvas, but I needed some space to breathe, so I walked up to my studio and put up my canvas there.

Today, my painting had all the colors possible—the brightest of shades and the darkest of nuances. It was pretty and ugly, happy and sad, comforting and painful, hopeful and hopeless, all at the same time.

It was her.

And no, I was not talking about Avni.

CHAPTER SIX

AVNI

The door was open when I walked into Vivaan's studio.

He was so engrossed in painting that he didn't even realize that I was standing behind him, and I didn't bother to announce my arrival. He was a different person when he painted; his actions were aggressive as he filled up every inch of his canvas. I wondered if he always painted with as much aggression or if this one was special. It was an intense painting— the face of a girl was hidden half behind her hair and half behind a mist and some random strokes. All I could see was her eyes that were partly wet with tears. It was not me. And it made me sad for some unknown reason.

When he finished the painting, he took a deep sigh as if it was exhausting and stared at his creation for a long time.

"Beautiful," I said, finally announcing my arrival.

He spun around, surprised. I loved his painter avatar—a brush in one hand, palette in the other, and little colorful splashes across his white T-shirt.

"Beautiful," he repeated.

"I am talking about the painting." I pointed at it.

"I am talking about you," he pointed at me, taking me off guard with his unexpected compliment.

"Is this how you talk to every girl?" Thankfully, I could throw out some words despite my heart beating at the speed of an express train. Today I was determined not to act stupid.

"I don't have many friends who are girls. Actually, I don't even have many friends."

"Are you kidding me? You have no girls as friends? I walked towards him.

"Why should that be a surprise?"

"Because someone as hot as you..." I clamped my mouth shut, feeling the heat travel up my neck. Damn! Why was it so difficult to behave normally around him?

A lopsided grin enveloped his face, making him even hotter, "do you talk like this to every boy?" he asked mischievously sending a tingle down my spine.

"Shut up!" I looked away. God, I was blushing. Would he be jealous if I talked to every boy like that? I almost asked him, but thank God, I stopped myself from acting stupid again.

"So, working hard for your next exhibition?" I quickly changed the topic and pointed at his painting. The way his body reacted while painting her, I was sure it was not merely his imagination. And I was jealous for sure.

"This is not for sale. This will go there too." He pointed at the storeroom and I realized there were many paintings there, neatly stacked vertically, facing the wall. The other day I was so busy admiring him, I missed watching the other paintings.

"Again?" My eyebrows shot up.

"Yeah." He shrugged his shoulder. "I shouldn't have. Now I will have to paint one more tonight."

"Are they also not for sale?" I pointed at the storeroom.

"Right. They are not."

"Do you mind if I see the other paintings?"

The expression on his face changed; his easy smile was gone. He slipped into a different personality suddenly, a sad and quiet version maybe. "I am sorry. I shouldn't have asked," I apologized.

"You don't need to be sorry. Follow me," he said and walked towards the storeroom and I followed him. Crammed together in his little space felt intimate, which made me more aware of his hotness. Like last time he pulled out a few paintings hovering above me, and I tried to stay unaffected by his exotic cologne and his proximity. I failed miserably.

When he showed me the paintings, I felt a pang in my heart. All the paintings were of girls, their faces were almost hidden by either hair or a flowing dupatta or a flying leaf, but the eyes reflected a strange emptiness in all of them. Strangely, they all resembled the painting he had just made. I noticed how his paintings reflected something that was close and yet elusive for him, but being so near to him I had lost my voice so I silently helped him put back the paintings on the shelf above before walking out.

It was quiet for a while. I wanted to ask who was that girl, because of course she wasn't just his imagination, but I couldn't voice my question. His expression was guarded, though through the cracks his hurt was visible. He knew I was trying to read him, so he cleared his throat and broke the silence, "It seems you didn't keep your promise. Where are your paintings?" He eyed my empty hands.

"I kept them there," I replied, thankful for the uncomfortable silence to end, and reached the bag I had dropped at the entrance. "Well, it was stupid of me to think that I should show you my immature paintings," I said, walking back to him as he settled on the couch.

"It's stupid to think this way. Now come on, show me your sketchbook." He commanded, forwarding his hand.

His commanding tone startled me, but I liked it. I gave him the sketchbook, hesitantly. He opened my sketchbook, and the first drawing was of colorful flowers in a vase.

"Nice, how old were you when you drew this?"

"Ten," I said, cursing myself for giving him my sketchbook. The drawing looked more immature after witnessing his art.

He turned the page and the second painting was of birds, the third one was of a butterfly. And so on...

The second last painting was of a doll. He traced his fingers over that painting as I had done over his, and then he stared at me. His gaze penetrated through my clothes and my skin and traveled straight up to my heart, which was now beating irrationally fast.

"You know what? We can lie to ourselves, we can lie to the people we love but we can never lie to our art." His eyes refused to leave mine.

His words touched the part of me that was not for the world to see. My parents raised me as a boy, for their own reasons. Dad disliked girls and mom thought girls were weak. And Avinash just followed the trend. But I think his reason somehow resonated the reasons of my mom. I hated all those reasons.

I and Avinash, wore the same type of clothes throughout our childhood and I was comfortable with that, but as I grew up things changed. While growing up, I wavered between my body that rebelled to be a girl and my mind that pushed me to act like a boy. Girls and boys were different—biologically, emotionally, mentally. It wasn't an issue of who was smarter, it was just that they were different. What I had become was a mess between a girl and a boy.

I wanted to pour myself out to him, about how tired I was to carry this trend any longer, how I always wanted a doll but ended up getting a football. And maybe, just maybe, I wanted to share with him the story behind the last painting...Cement, bricks...But I just couldn't utter a word. He was a stranger, even though he didn't feel like one. Wasn't it scary? Before he turned the page to that last painting, I hastily pulled the book away from his hand.

"That's all," I mumbled when that was not all. Before he could ask me anything else, I continued, "about what you said...your art also says a lot about you."

"Like?" The way he stared at me without blinking made me nervous. I should have told him not to look at me like that.

"You are running away from the same thing you are running towards." The girl in those paintings touched a raw nerve in him, yet he couldn't stop painting her.

His body shifted a little, his emotions losing their guard once again. An emotion passed his face as he stared at me, at the storeroom, at the different paintings in the room, and back towards me.

He opened his mouth to say something, but my stupid phone spoiled the moment with its stupid ringtone.

Re mama, re mama, re mama re...

Shit. I made a mental note to check my ringtone before I entered Vivaan's studio next time.

"Yes, Avinash, yes. I am reaching in fifteen minutes." I said into the phone. "I told you I went for a walk." Oh shit! I was stupid and I should have accepted it without trying to change the fact. Now Vivaan knew I lied at home to meet him. I disconnected the phone, "Umm...sorry I need to leave. I am late." I said, not meeting his eyes.

"Sure, it's already late for a walk." He smiled, and I couldn't help but smile back.

"Shut up," I hit him on his arm.

"So, when are you going for the next walk?" he teased, as I was leaving the studio.

"Tomorrow, most probably," I replied before walking out, and I couldn't stop smiling until I reached home, but my smile vanished the moment I stepped inside my home.

He was back.

Dad.

CHAPTER SEVEN

VIVAAN

"Broken and hidden."

"You are running away from the same thing you are running towards."

Every word of hers found a way to my soul as if it knew the path as if I was connected to her long before we met.

Connection...yes, a nice topic for my next painting.

I was tired, but the memory of Arjun's hunched-up frame kept pushing me. He was the only friend I had since I was ten. I still remembered the first day we met at school. Every eye that gazed my way reflected either pity or disgust, but Arjun was different. Even at that age he was more sensitive than most people and got into endless fights whenever someone mocked me. As time passed, I became immune to the senseless remarks of people, but not him.

I looked at my watch. It must be his dinner break, so I called him and we decided to meet at the tea joint beneath his call center.

The place was busy and Arjun was waiting for me, with two cups of piping hot tea on the table, as usual. I took my seat and gave him the box of his favorite *besan laddus* mom packed for him.

"I am starving." He opened the box and started gobbling the laddus. When I tried to take one, he pulled the box closer to him. "You can eat it at your home."

I smiled at his gesture and took a sip of my tea. I liked the traces of the old Arjun in this renewed version. Only once he finished all the *laddus* did he take a breath.

"Huh, feeling better now." He closed the lid and returned the box. We talked casually for a while before he suddenly exclaimed, "Oh shit! I forgot to purchase dad's medicines. How could I? He can't miss his night dose."

"Give me the prescription. I will get the medicines and give them to him on my way home."

As he pulled out the prescription from his wallet, his mother's photo slipped out from it. His gaze lingered on her photo before he kept it back and fumbled for money, but there wasn't much in his wallet.

"Your break must be over, I should leave." I said placing the empty tea cup on the table, "I will give him medicines on my way back home." We didn't talk about money, but the hint of embarrassment on his face as he nodded, broke me. I knew how much he hated getting help, but there should be no place for embarrassment with your own people. I realized for the first time why mom hated it whenever I got conscious about asking something from them.

I looked at his face one more time and it hurt me to see the pain etched all over his features. He was nowhere near the Arjun I knew. I remember his mother always scolded him for how irresponsible he was. She hated his laziness and often told him, "Learn something from Vivaan."

"Why don't you adopt him if he is so good," he would snap back, getting possessive like a five-year-old. His mother would shrug her shoulder looking at me, and we just laughed at his gesture.

He lost her to an accident last year, and it completely changed Arjun. Whatever was left of him was taken away by his dad's illness. His whole personality had changed. After his mother's death, he used to lose his temper easily, but now he was too tired to even be angry. If his mother was alive, she would be so proud of her son who was working nonstop, juggling his studies, his job, and also taking care of his ailing father.

As I walked back, I thought of different ways I could try to earn more money. Maybe I could take up the ghost-writing opportunity offered by my professor. The money was less, but every penny counted. I restructured my schedule to fit in the writing.

CHAPTER EIGHT

AVNI

It took less than a second for my mind to swing from joy to doom to fear. Dad was home. Wasn't he supposed to return from his business tour next week?

"Why is Avni not home yet?" He banged his fist on the table, his back towards the door. Mom standing next to him, cringed at his volume. Anger overruled fear when it came to Avinash. His fist was tight and his eyes were red when his eyes shot up to me.

"Dad, I am here." I whimpered and he spun around.

"Do you know what time it is?" He thundered, "where were you?".

"On...on a night walk."

"Night walk? Since when did you start this so called..." his tone changed, and he mimicked my voice, "night walk?"

Standing behind dad, Avinash showed me his first finger but before I could make out anything, dad yelled, "Avni, I asked you something." He stomped towards me and with every step he took in my direction, my heartbeat quickened.

"Today was just...just...the se...second day, Dad."

"Second day?" his voice rose as he stared hard at mom. "Second day? Are you suffering from amnesia? You said she went out for the first time."

Damn! That's what Avinash gestured.

"Dad, actually..."

"Shut up, Avni," he screamed, staring at me, then Avinash and finally his cold gaze rested on mom. "What games are you all playing behind my back? Lying to me all the time."

"No dad, it's...it's actually..."

"Go to your room!" Dad cut my sentence midway, still staring at mom.

"But dad..."

"I said, go to your room." His gaze narrowed at mom and the same fear grabbed me again.

"Dad, please, at least..." I stepped towards him.

Now!" He shouted at the top of his voice and this time his dreadful eyes focused on me. All the courage I had mustered to save mom withered with his look and I reached the stairs.

"You need to be told separately?" he yelled at Avinash.

Avinash followed me to my room and started pacing up and down.

"Why didn't you tell me over the phone?" I asked him amid my sobs.

"Dad was standing right next to me."

And we heard it again. The sound that was a permanent companion of our childhood but became less apparent as dad started touring for his business. The sound of the belt on skin, and the muffled screams.

"I am sorry mom. I am so sorry." I murmured, rocking back and forth on my bed, trying to hold the tears that were flowing ceaselessly.

"Be strong, Avni." Avinash sat next to me and stroked my hair. "Don't be like her. Ever. Don't ever let any man harm you." He hugged me "Promise me, Avni."

"I promise, Avinash. And you don't ever be like him. Ever. Don't ever harm any woman. Promise me, Avinash.

"I promise."

Avinash soothed me until I was calm, and he stayed with me until he was sure that I was fine. He had always been the rock of my fragile world. Every suffering had to cross him before reaching me, except the sounds coming from our parent's room.

After a horrible incident seven years ago, mom made us promise to never intervene in their matters, though I feared we wouldn't be able to keep that promise for long.

Next morning, dad was in a wonderful mood. Of course, he had to be, his anger had got a good outlet. While sipping his tea he asked for his suitcase and when mom gave it to him, he pulled out a saree from it and lovingly draped it around my mother's shoulders. "Doesn't she look beautiful? I still love you as I did when I saw you first." His dimples were accentuated as he smiled. I inherited the dimples from him. I hope I didn't inherit anything else. People said his smile was enigmatic. I wondered if they were right. Maybe that's why mom stuck to him despite everything.

No. I knew it was a lie. She had stuck to him because of me.

CHAPTER NINE

VIVAAN

The college ended an hour earlier as our professor was on leave. I stopped at the nearby orphanage on my way home. Earlier, I used to visit every weekend with dad, but dad had constantly been working for months and even I was buried in my studies, paintings, and ghost-writing assignments. The moment I stepped inside, a calm rushed over me. The kids were playing in the park, but the moment they saw me they all ran towards me, and we all sat under the shade of a banyan tree, our favorite spot. I distributed chocolates to them and told them the story I had already told them more than a hundred times, but they still listened with the same curiosity. Their smiles always soothed my mind, but not today. I walked out, still feeling restless.

I went home and ate my favorite aloo paratha and for once I was done with all the assignments on time. I had promised Kanha that I'll play with him with his new car set and I did that. Playing with him always lightened up my mood, but I was still feeling a sense of emptiness.

I walked to the studio and tried mixing different colors, but I couldn't concentrate. After wasting a canvas with useless strokes, I tried to put up another. I couldn't think of anything to draw. I closed my eyes for inspiration and I saw her...Avni.

I snapped open my eyes. Where was this going? Was it even possible to miss someone after meeting them only three times? I stared at my paintings crowding the storeroom.

It was possible to miss someone even if you didn't know how they look...

I tried to focus and drew a boy waiting at a crossroad. The red light was blinking bright and the green light had a crack, the slightest, that might not be visible to an unobservant eye. As I subconsciously drew the crack, Avni's words reverberated in my mind—broken and hidden. Would she find the crack in this painting? Why she didn't come to visit me after that day? Why did I wait for her every day since then? Why did I feel my paintings were not complete until she brushed her fingers through them, when in fact, I hated anyone touching my paintings?

With each passing day, my hope withered and my heart felt an overwhelming sadness I wasn't aware I could feel.

After a few weeks my second art exhibition was up. The crowd was enormous this time. People appreciated the art hanging on the walls, but no one went beyond the hues, patterns, color combinations, and aesthetic value. People appreciated my art, but nobody understood it.

Not the way Avni did.

Soon, I stopped eavesdropping on people's conversations regarding my art. I just wanted to know what Avni would have thought about the paintings. Someone pulled my kurta and as I looked down, a surprise awaited me.

"Kanha!" I chuckled. He climbed on my lap. "Bhaiya, you drew all these paintings?" he pointed his finger at a painting and then throughout the room.

I nodded, and he complained, "You have time to paint so much, but not to play with me? I am not going to talk to you." He folded his hands in mock anger.

"I am sorry." I held my ear with my free hand. "I will play with your new toy set tonight. Promise."

He opened his palm and I kept my hand on his tiny one. "Gentleman's promise."

"Yay!" He raised his fist in victory, got down, and ran towards Arjun.

I turned towards mom and dad. "Dad, you had an important meeting today, didn't you?"

"Not more important than your exhibition. We couldn't even make it to your last exhibition as I wasn't in town and Kanha was ill, so of course, this time we had to come."

"I am proud of you." Mom stepped closer and touched my chin. She didn't look upset anymore that I was pushing my boundaries. I held her hand on my chin. Her approval meant a lot to me.

After a little while, dad asked, "Waiting for someone?" it was then I realized that my gaze was constantly returning to the entrance.

"No," I lied.

CHAPTER TEN

AVNI

I didn't leave the house apart from going to college since dad returned. Some days passed by peacefully. Dad told mom not to work so hard and took us out for dinner. He acted like the hero I always wanted him to be. But some days God knows what ignited his anger. He could get angry at the slightest thing like the dal was burnt or the vegetable was too salty. One day, he rang the bell and mom was in the bathroom and we didn't know, so we didn't get down to open the door. Within a few seconds, he started ringing the bell frantically. I rushed downstairs from my room and mom came out from the washroom. As soon as she opened the door, dad entered and slapped mom so hard, she tumbled back.

"Where were you, bitch?"

"I...I was in the washroom." Mom's voice trembled with pain or fear, or maybe both.

"Where are your kids? Haven't you taught them anything?"

I dared not enter their conversation. Dad never hit us. I mean, never after we grew up. As kids he used to hit us, especially he used to hit Avinash a lot. We tried not to do anything that annoyed him. The only problem was that sometimes we just couldn't predict what would annoy him. Sometimes, I thought it wasn't even our fault, he carried his anger from the office.

Now he was on a tour most of the time and we liked it that way. We laughed a lot when he wasn't around and there was a sense of normalcy. Though there was no normalcy in admitting that we were happy when our father was not around.

I ran back to my room. One look at my face and Avinash knew it.

"Did he hit her again?"

I nodded. His eyes were bloodshot when he hit the wall with his fist. When we were kids, we used to cry whenever their shouting pierced our room and our childhood, but as we grew up, Avinash's pain gave way to anger bit by bit. Sometimes he would throw things around. Sometimes he punched the wall, sometimes he made his fist so tight that his nails were buried in his skin. His feelings had taken a violent form and that scared me. More than his anger, Dad's reflection in Avinash scared me.

"I will teach that bastard a lesson today." His voice was low but the tone was throat-cutting as he walked out of the door.

"Avinash, wait." I held his hand. "He is our father, you can't hit him."

He tried to get out of my grip but stopped as soon as tears trickled down my cheeks. My tears were his weakness and I hated crying in his presence, but sometimes I just couldn't help it.

"Don't cry Avni. Don't be like her." He drew me in his arms like I was a small kid and stoked the back of my head.

What would I have done without him? He was the only vibrant hue of my turbulent childhood and the only hope of my difficult youth.

A muffled scream reached my ears and I fisted Avinash's T-shirt.

Mom should have left him.

There was a time mom used to fight back, shout and scream and even try to hit dad back, but her fragile body was no match for his huge build. Mom was a strong woman. Strong enough to raise her kids alone and she was ready for a divorce but then I made one mistake. One big mistake that changed everything.

That night mom changed. Never again did she try to fight back, and the fights ended soon with the sound of only some snuffling and a few whippings reaching our ears. It was better than all the shouting and name-calling that would continue for hours. Did I say it was better? What a pathetic daughter I was!

"Avinash," Dad's shrill voice cut through my reverie. "Avinash, come down," Dad shouted.

His hands were still folded in a fist as he walked downstairs.

"This bloody remote control stopped working. Go and get cells from the market."

Avinash's gait was aggressive when he took the money from dad. Thankfully, dad was focused on the television.

"Dad, can I also go?" I badly needed some air to breathe.

Dad stared hard at me and I regretted my question. But then he nodded.

How was it possible that the weather outside was so pleasant, how was it that the spring was on the onset? And how was it that I hated it?

Mom needed this fresh air more than me.

Vivaan's studio was on the way and it was crowded, as it was his exhibition. I had missed him, though I didn't know how was it possible to miss someone after just three meetings.

"What happened, why did you stop?" Avinash turned towards me when I lagged.

"I want to see this exhibition." More than the exhibition, I wanted to see him.

"You are in the mood to see an art exhibition?" His eyebrows shot up.

How could I explain, that was the only thing I was in a mood to do? I nodded, not meeting his eyes.

"Whatever!" He turned his back to me and walked towards the market.

I looked down at my clothes. I hadn't even bothered to change before leaving. I combed my hair with my fingers and tried to straighten the wrinkles on my shirt with my hands before walking inside.

My eyes searched the length and breadth of his gallery, but it wasn't difficult to spot him. He stood out from the crowd in his traditional white kurta and blue jeans. His large hands were folded against his chest and he was nodding to someone. My heart had started to scare me due to its irrational beating every time I saw him. I was about to call out his name when my phone started ringing. It wasn't a ridiculous ringtone this time, but it was loud enough to gain attention. My knees buckled up on seeing dad's name flashing on the screen. With trembling fingers, I pressed the green button.

"Avni, also bring a pack of mouth freshener."

"Okay," I barely said.

"Why is Avinash not picking up his phone? Pass on the phone to him."

My hands dampened, and my voice choked. I pressed the mute button realizing the light music in the background might make him suspicious.

It was when I turned around to leave that I heard Vivaan's voice calling out my name.

Have you ever felt too many emotions by just listening to your name?

I did at that moment as I ignored his voice and ran outside his studio. I heard music in his voice. He called again, and I heard concern. He called again, and I heard despair.

I ran up to Avinash and tapped his shoulder from behind and in between my gasps, I managed to say "Dad." I wanted to look back once at Vivaan. Just once. But somehow, I couldn't gather the courage with all the tears flowing down my cheeks.

He wasn't calling me anymore. And in that silence, I heard a crash. Of his trust breaking into pieces.

CHAPTER ELEVEN

VIVAAN

"Avni," I called her, but she didn't even look my way and turned away from the entrance itself. I rushed to the entrance and called her again, but she was running away as if she was participating in a race. I kept on calling her until mom's hand landed on my shoulder. I spun around to find all the eyes staring at me.

"Who is she?" mom asked, studying my face.

"A friend," I breathed, but the way mom kept on staring at my face, I knew she didn't trust me. I pushed my hands in my pocket and walked towards one of my paintings trying to avoid the stares of my family, and the strangers around, also trying to escape my own feelings.

Maybe I was thinking too much about her. Maybe she came to my exhibition just as an afterthought. Maybe I should have tried and focused on people who were there to support me rather than who walked away. I reached the couple looking at one of the paintings of the sky, trying to focus on their reaction, but I failed to hear a thing they said. Somewhere in my mind, Avni was rolling her fingers over the golden and amber hues of the sky painting, her husky voice told me of the hairline crack in the setting sun. I jerked myself out of the trance in time. Thankfully, I was skilled at diverting my mind from things or people. I had learned that skill too early in my life. I had to.

But there were always exceptions.

Despite earning way more than what I expected, a feeling of discontent washed over me as I walked home.

Avni never turned up after that day. I recalled our last meeting umpteen times to remember if I had said something wrong, but I didn't remember a thing. She had looked happy and I thought she enjoyed my company. I was probably stupid.

Wasn't it strange how we refused to believe in things we never experienced? I never believed in love at first sight. No, I wasn't hinting, that I was in love. Love was a complex emotion, but yes, I felt a strange sense of emptiness in her absence. I felt like my heart was an empty canvas waiting to be painted in myriad nuances and somehow, I felt no one but Avni could fill those colors.

As days passed her thoughts stopped teasing me nonstop, but her memories still came in waves, washing over me in a moment and leaving me the next.

One evening, when I was painting a lone bird flying high in a sky tainted by a dozen hues of setting sun, a husky voice whispered my name.

"Vivaan."

My name in that voice unbalanced my heart, and I waited for my beats to calm down before turning back to face her.

"Avni." I tried to keep my voice neutral. "After a long time."

"Yeah," she nodded. "Just wanted to see your latest art, if you don't mind," she mumbled.

"Of course, I expected you at my exhibitions."

"Sorry, got a little busy." She avoided my gaze and reached my painting. She traced her fingers over it and a strange sense of satisfaction washed over me.

"This is so beautiful. The lone bird searching for a companion, struggling alone in the vast, empty sky. But I guess she is tired, I mean this bird, the way her wings are giving up." Her eyes ran up and down the painting, surpassing the mundane details and delving deeper into the art.

She kept speaking as if to herself, "See this sky, subdued in so many colors. The way one nuance envelops the other so that no one can see what's the core of it." Her eyes glistened, as her words faded into silence and her fingers stopped midway.

"Are you okay?" I asked, stepping towards her.

"I am fine," she blinked.

"You have lost a lot of weight."

"I have six months to recoup." She immediately bit her lip as if she regretted saying it.

"Why six months?"

She was quiet for a while, maybe thinking of a reason that wasn't the truth. "You know, I keep saying stupid things!" She forced a smile that didn't reach her eyes.

"Come with me." I held her hand and though it was an innocent act, her touch lefts its imprints in my heart just the way it did on my paintings. I led her to the couch and we settled on it, a little too close. She didn't attempt to make any distance and I wasn't sure I could stay focused, but I didn't attempt to move away. The lights were dim but the sadness in her eyes was unmistakable, and this was when she wasn't even looking at me.

"Are you ok?"

She nodded, still looking at the floor.

"What kept you busy for so long?"

"Got a little busy with my assignments," she said, her gaze fixed to the ground.

She wasn't a good liar, but I didn't tell her that. I decided to get to the core by changing the topic.

"You understand my art so well. I also observed something about your art, by the way."

"What?" She looked at me for the first time today.

"You painted the doll that you probably never got. You painted all the pretty flowers and birds in pink and red. Maybe your favorite colours. I never saw you wearing those colors." I didn't add that I often imagined her in a flowing red gown and how lovely she looked in that imaginary dress.

"It was a long time ago," she said defensively as if she didn't want to talk about it.

"It might be. On the surface you might have changed, but," I hesitated, "I am talking about the core. The core of you." I pointed at her heart.

"I don't know what you are talking about." The way she got up defensively, I knew I had hit the right spot.

"What's stopping you, Avni?" I got up with her. "The way one nuance envelops the other so that no one can see it." I reiterated her own words. "You weren't talking about the painting, you were talking about you. The way your tomboyish image hides the soft, sensitive girl beneath. Why are you so scared of her? Why Avni?"

"Because I don't want to be like her." Avni's voice cracked, and she abruptly turned away, "because I don't want to be like her." she repeated before she vanished out of my studio.

Who was this *her* that Avni was talking about?

CHAPTER TWELVE

AVNI

I was gasping for breath when I reached home. I had run all the way. I was running away from Vivaan, from the truth he said, from everyone and everything. I was probably running away from myself too.

'The way one nuance envelops the other so that no one can see it.' Yes, I was that painting. I was a girl who was trying hard to hide it all. That night, when my feelings weren't painted in any of the fake colors, was dark and ugly. Seven years had passed, and layers of several seasons had covered it, but sometimes, I thought there was a hole, a big ugly hole in the layers of time through which the past crawled straight to my heart. Every time I heard a belt whipping across flesh, the hole got wider, allowing the past to rush forth with such force that I lost my balance.

I wiped out my tears before entering my home. Avinash was removing his wristwatch and keeping it in the drawer beneath the television stand. Maybe he also just returned from somewhere, with that bag in his hand.

When mom walked out of the kitchen, her face looked free from fear after a long time. Only after fear left its traces did it allow the pain to sneak in.

Avinash turned and when he saw me, he said, "Mom, have you ever seen a grown-up boy crying? Doesn't it look silly?" He teased me.

No, it's not silly. I have seen you crying, albeit without tears.

"First, I am not a boy and second, I wasn't crying." I knew he was teasing me for a reason—to curb the scary silence dad had left for us.

"Whatever," he shrugged his shoulders and laid down his bag on the table. He pulled out a vada pav for mom, her favorite, and handed me a packet of noodles. "Earthworms for you," he joked.

My hand dangled midway before I could take it from him. "Yuck, why do you always have to say that? I am not going to eat it now." I took my hand back and folded them defensively.

He opened the parcel and lifted a single noodle in the air. "Look, mom, doesn't it look like an earthworm?" He threw that noodle at me.

The next moment, he was on the floor and I was hitting him with a pillow and mom was warning us to clear the mess ourselves and stop fighting like we were in kindergarten. And soon, the silence dad had left behind himself was replaced by chaos. Beautiful, peaceful chaos.

That night I couldn't sleep for a very long time. The way Avinash had laughed so hard that he became teary-eyed during the pillow fight, I knew those were the tears he had stopped from flowing for too long. He just needed an excuse to free them. He was hurting too, but like every other time, he was the one to bring back smiles into our lives. I walked to his room and he was already asleep. I tousled his hair and returned to my room.

I woke up late the next day. Avinash shouted from his room, "Don't get late, I am not going to wait for you if you get late. Okay?"

"It's you who's always late, not me. Okay?" I shouted back.

Mom shouted from the kitchen, "Stop fighting and get down. Your breakfast is getting cold."

And within forty-five minutes we were at college, five minutes late, accusing each other as we entered the class. The day dragged by amid boring lectures and finally, we walked to the canteen during the break.

We still had twenty minutes after we finished our lunch, so I planned to visit the library rather than get bored by the cricket match conversation of Avinash and his friends.

I didn't want to go to the library, but neither did I want to go with the girls. God, where did I want to go?

I wasn't expecting God to reply so soon.

Vivaan.

He was walking across the road with Arjun, my classmate. Arjun was in his studio that night, so I should have known he knew Vivaan. Gosh! I behaved so stupidly last night that it was best to hide away, and with that thought, I slid behind the nearest tree.

"Hey, Avni." Vivaan walked up to me.

"Hi," I stepped out.

"Why were you hiding behind that tree?"

Shit! Was it that obvious? To say I was embarrassed would be an understatement. I had to speak out. Something...anything.

"I like the trunk of this tree." Shit!

Vivaan didn't smile like he always did when I goofed up, he just kept staring at me with a hint of concern in his eyes. I couldn't look into them anymore so I averted my gaze.

Thankfully, he changed the topic.

"You study here?"

"Yeah, I am in the second year of electrical engineering." I pointed to the right side of the road to our department.

"She is my classmate," Arjun said.

"Oh, I didn't know that, I study journalism," Vivaan said. He looked like a perfect journalist in his white kurta and blue jeans. He pointed in the direction of his class. "It's on the other side of that building."

Our university was huge, with almost eighty courses, ranging from Medicine to commerce running across five campuses. Each campus was connected with the other through a magnificent garden.

"Hey, you guys continue," Arjun glanced at his wristwatch, "I will catch you later."

We bid him goodbye and continued with the conversation, "Never saw you before." He said.

"We might have crossed paths, but we didn't know each other earlier." I didn't add that it felt like I had known him for years.

"Maybe. I am starving. Want to join me?" Vivaan pointed at the canteen.

I glanced at my watch. Avinash must have left the canteen by now. "Okay," I said.

I did a quick check before stepping into the canteen. Thankfully, Avinash had left.

"Tea or coffee?" he asked me when we reached the counter.

"Tea." I was already full. Where would this tea land?

"What else?" he asked me.

"Nothing. Already had my lunch."

He ordered something, and we walked to one of the side tables.

"Why were you alone? Where are your friends?" He asked as soon as we sat down.

"You mean Avinash and Shreyansh? Avinash is my twin brother and Shreyansh is Avinash's friend more than he is mine." I hoped my expressions didn't turn sour at Shreyansh's name. "I was getting bored by their talks, so I just walked out," I said blatantly.

"You always talk your mind?" He grinned, stretching his back in the chair that was too small for him.

I nodded. "Something most people can't take."

"So, we have something in common." He grinned at me and my gaze lingered at his perfect smile. The lights in his studio had been dim. Here, in broad daylight, I got a good look at his face. His skin was tanned, his dark hair needed a haircut, but it added a boyish charm to his mature look and I liked it. There was a small cleft on his jaw, his lips were just perfect as the rest of his rugged features and when my gaze traveled to his eyes, I gasped. He had caught me wandering over his features. Or did I catch him staring at me? I wasn't sure, but a flutter rose in my stomach and I broke the eye lock. Thankfully, our order arrived before the situation could turn awkward.

He had ordered fritters, samosa, chat, and paratha. And of course, tea. I could survive on all that food for a week.

"I eat a lot." He smiled.

Damn! Was I so easily readable? "Of course, for that macho body, this might be less."

He took a sip of the hot tea and said, "Who else is in your family apart from Avinash?".

"My mom." I cupped the tea between my palms. "And dad, but dad is mostly out on business tours."

"Is he on a tour now?" he slid the plate towards me, offering me the fritters.

"Yes, for six months"

I have six months to recoup. Shit.

Our eyes met for a brief second as his hand dangled midway with the tea in his hand. Ignoring the obvious question in his eyes, I changed the topic.

"Who all are in your family?" I picked a fritter to avoid looking at his eyes.

"Mom, dad, and Kanha, my four-year-old brother."

"Four years!"

"Yeah, he is nineteen years younger than me."

That meant he was twenty-three, four years older than me. He should have graduated by now.

"Your mom works?" I asked, picking up another fritter.

"Yup, she is a freelancer. And dad is a businessman and also a counselor."

"Counsellor! Wow. So, you needn't go anywhere else when you are stressed out."

"The thing is, they never let me get stressed out." Pride reflected on his face as he talked about his parents.

A pang of jealousy hit me, but then I was jealous of everyone who considered their parents as their role models. How long did I try to be like my parents? How many times did I fail? And two weak voices appeared out of nowhere.

Don't be like her.

Don't be like him.

"What happened? Where are you lost?" Vivaan waved his hand in front of me.

"I am here." I offered a weak smile "Hey, you drank your tea real fast. I haven't yet started. It's still so hot."

"Don't worry, take your time. We shouldn't be the same in everything."

I couldn't make out what he meant by that, but his smile was captivating and I was smiling at him without knowing.

He didn't ask me why I ran away abruptly last night. I was glad but also disappointed that he didn't bother. As I glanced around, I knew the place was small and the conversation from one table could be heard at the others. Maybe that's why he didn't get into an intense conversation as he did in his studio.

Once ready to leave, we exchanged phone numbers and as I waved him goodbye, he asked, "Planning to go for a night walk today?" His eyes glinted with hope.

"Maybe."

What was about this smiling every time we talked?

CHAPTER THIRTEEN

VIVAAN

Avni came for a walk that night and the nights that followed. I never asked her why she left abruptly that night, not because I didn't care but because I didn't want to make her uncomfortable. Earlier she talked only a little but as she opened up, I saw a whole new side to her. Generally, she was the one who did all the talking and I was glad since I was not much of a talker. And God, she was a chatterbox! She could talk about anything ranging from what she ate in the afternoon to why Newton invented so many laws. She lived in a different world far away from reality and I loved it. There were times I couldn't follow her words. I just saw the way her eyes glinted, the way her dimple deepened, the way her nose flinched, the way she jumped in her seat, the way she asked for a clap when she was happy. Her little gestures of innocence were traveling straight to my heart. Was she aware of what she was doing to me?

She was in my studio again, wearing her usual jeans and T-shirt, with a denim jacket. We were sitting on the couch and she was twitching her fingers, something she did when she was upset.

"What's the matter?" I asked, and she replied so fast as if she was just waiting for me to ask.

"Look," she pulled out her mobile from her jeans pocket and shifted towards me so hastily that she almost bumped into me.

"Oops, sorry!" She pulled back and I couldn't help but notice how her face flushed and she struggled to breathe. She tried to shift her attention to the mobile, but I couldn't. Her touch had sent shivers down my spine and thankfully, I was skilled at masking my emotions. We both stared into the mobile to avoid the obvious awkwardness.

It was a snapshot of news. A kid had been rescued from child traffickers and he was narrating his story. His voice was unsteady and though he was in safe hands, fear had not yet left its traces.

"They kidnapped me from my home and took me to an unknown place I knew nothing about. They gave me only four pieces of bread or a handful of biscuits to eat in the whole day. I was always hungry. Sometimes I ate leftover food from the dustbins, and they would beat me if I didn't bring any money."

He lifted his shirt with his right hand and showed the scars. His eyes were vacant, with no hint of innocence, those eyes had seen more than their fair share.

"Then one day they..." His voice trailed away and he didn't finish the statement, instead, he brought forward his left hand, mutilated. The journalist took over the mike and dramatically spoke things that weren't considerate for the kid but were maybe good for TRP.

"Maybe a seven-year-old innocent boy with ragged clothes, disheveled hair, and a body that was no more than a bundle of bones wasn't pitiable. They thought he wasn't supposed to be loved, he was supposed to be pitied. The scars on his soul will never heal. He will never be the same again."

I got up abruptly from the sofa while the video was still playing. "It happens, Avni." I blurted, unable to avoid my sudden disconnect. I needed air so I walked up to the open door, but the breeze did nothing to calm down my raging nerves.

The journalist was still mumbling, "The poor kid must have feared life more than death." Thankfully, Avni closed the video before I had to ask her to do it. The silence between us grew thick. It was in such moments I realized that she was the only one who kept our communication going.

I knew she expected something more than 'it happens', maybe some expression of disgust or some words of comfort, but I failed to give any. When I turned back to face her, she was looking at me like I was the most heartless person in the world. A video that would make most people cringe couldn't get any reaction out of me. She opened her mouth to say something but then her gaze briefly traveled to my hands folded at my chest and she didn't say anything. I wasn't sure if I looked intimidating or inaccessible, because, like Avni, most people backed out when I was in that position.

She left early that night, but I didn't stop her. Days passed and then one day, she was humming, and when I asked her why, she said she had witnessed something beautiful.

"While returning from college I saw an injured puppy. I walked towards him, but before I could reach him a woman got down from a big car and lifted him. She wasn't scared that her clothes will get ruined. When I asked her what she would do with it, she said she would take the puppy to a vet and then she will keep it with her. Isn't that sweet?" she chuckled. I just smiled, disappointing her again. She was untouched by this ruthless world, and I wished it always remained that way. It didn't take her much to cry or laugh, her one trait that was opposite from me and something that pulled me towards her.

There were days I felt connected and there were days I felt disconnected, not only from her but from the world around me in general. But with each passing day, the periods of disconnection were fading. Avni was awakening the parts of me that died along with my childhood, and I wasn't sure if it was good or bad.

It was almost five months since we were meeting at my studio and the college. One day, upon getting no reaction from me after showing me a ruthless video, she asked me, "nothing affects you?"

"I have seen so much of beauty and ugliness in this world that I am now unperturbed by either."

Her gaze traveled straight to the paintings in the storeroom and she knew either the beauty I had seen or the ugliness I had witnessed was related to the girl in the painting. Was she right? I didn't know.

"Can I ask you something?" she hesitated.

"Go ahead."

"Who...I mean...Who is..." She twitched her lips, "who is—"

"Speak, Avni," I looked straight into her eyes.

"Who's that girl?" She pointed at the storeroom.

It was a difficult question and I didn't want to go there. But I didn't want to lie to her as well, so I settled for something between a truth and a lie. "My imagination." I tried to keep my voice stable.

"All your paintings are your imagination and you sell them, but you never sell those paintings."

A half-lie was more than enough. She deserved the truth, but I was not ready to talk about it. "I don't want to discuss it." My tone was blunt and the hurt on her face was evident. "I am sorry, Avni, but you know that I speak my mind." My voice was softer now but she was already hurt.

"It's ok, I shouldn't have asked. It should be none of my business," she said, clearly disappointed in me.

"No, it's not that, Avni." I touched her hand.

"Yes, it's that only." She pulled back. "I thought we were friends and friends share everything."

"Even you don't share everything." She shared all the videos of the world with me but nothing about why she missed my exhibition, why she ran away abruptly that day from my studio, what was it about her dad that in his absence she could recoup.

"You might judge me," she mumbled. I never judged people and I was sure even without knowing the reason I could never judge her.

"So might you," I snapped back. "But frankly, it doesn't matter if someone judges me. It's just that I don't want to discuss it."

I was blunt again, though I tried to be softer, I couldn't fake it.

"Okay, I should leave now. I have some assignments to complete." She was fast to change the topic, but not fast enough to veil the hurt and embarrassment. She got up and turned to leave.

"Avni wait. You misunderstood me." I held her hand, trying to ignore how her little hand fit in mine, "I didn't mean..."

She turned her head to look at me, "You have said all that you mean, Vivaan." She pulled her hand out of my grip and walked away.

I wanted to stop her, but it was late, and I didn't know what to tell her. I wasn't much of a confrontational person either. Maybe someday I would tell her what she thought mattered.

She mattered...like no one ever did.

And for the first time in years, I felt the need to be expressive, to inculcate the gentleness, a girl like Avni deserved. When my phone beeped with a message I expected it to bring some welcome distraction, but it further heightened the turmoil I had been feeling.

"Tomorrow 9.00 PM, Bluestar Hotel, Delhi. I might not be able to chase her anymore; this is your last chance. She might stay there for a while, but I am not sure."

The phone trembled in my hand. Tomorrow? How could I reach there so soon? What would I say to mom and dad?

I hurled the phone on the couch and paced in my studio trying to get a grip on all the conflicting emotions cluttering my mind. Hadn't I waited for this moment all my life? Then why was I so scared of facing it? Why I still felt unprepared, and yet couldn't wait for the moment of coming face to face with her.

I locked the studio, and walked back home tyring to tame down the demons of my heart. I entered in and for the first time, I was glad that the door was unlocked. I could avoid mom for a few more minutes. But I was wrong.

"How many times did I tell you to finish your dinner and then you can go wherever you want but you never listen to me."

"Sorry, mom." I avoided looking at her.

"What happened, Vivaan?" Her voice mellowed down as she walked in front of me.

"Nothing. I will go get fresh." I walked to my room without looking at her. When I returned after freshening up, mom and dad were waiting at the table for me. I glanced at the wall clock; it was ten in the night. I shouldn't have kept them waiting for so long.

"What happened? Anything bothering you?" Dad asked when he saw me staring at my plate.

What could I tell him? He always taught us that communication was the key, there was no place for secrets in a family, but my truth had the power to disturb the very foundation of our family so I had no option, but to keep my secret.

"Dad, I will stay at Arjun's place tomorrow," I didn't look up from the plate but I felt his gaze on me.

"Okay, is his dad fine?"

"Yes, but I think Arjun needs me." It was easier to lie when I wasn't looking at them.

"Sure, no problem."

I looked up and dad had resumed eating. Mom was still staring at me, with something unreadable in her eyes, but she didn't say anything. I was expecting a few questions, but none came and I pushed aside the thought that something was wrong. I gulped down my food and after resigning to my room I booked a 10.00 AM flight to Delhi for the next day. Then I called Arjun.

"Arjun, I need your help. I am staying at your place tomorrow, but just for the records. That is what you are going to tell my parents if there is ever any need."

It was quiet for a while, obviously, he needed time to take in this shift in my personality.

"That's not a big deal," he said finally, "but hey, what's going on?"

"Nothing to worry about."

"Some girl?"

"You know me better!"

"Of course, I was just kidding." His tone shifted from teasing to concern. "All well?"

"Yup," I said, and he knew nothing more was coming from me.

I lied down on the bed and the second hand of the clock dragged, a total contrast to my mind. After an eternity, when the morning alarm rang—which I didn't need anyway because I was already awake—the feeling of guilt was still eating at me.

It was just seven when I was ready to leave.

"You are leaving so early?" Mom asked as soon as I stepped out of my room.

"Yeah, have to discuss an assignment with a friend before the class starts," I said, walking towards the shoe rack, not looking at her. Damn. I was behaving like a habitual liar.

"At least eat your breakfast." Mom said, but today her tone was more of a request than her usual commanding tone.

"I am getting late. I will eat something at the canteen." I was tying my shoelace and finally, when I looked at mom's face, the look in her eyes broke my heart. She was looking tired; her hair was disheveled and the natural enthusiasm on her face was missing. I walked up to her and asked, "Are you ok?" I touched her forehead; she wasn't ill.

"Yes, Kanha was up last night," she said, eyeing the floor.

I was up all night too. If Kanha was up, it was impossible that I didn't hear his voice. Why was she lying?

She looked up at me and we communicated something in silence. We both were lying and we both knew that, but we feared asking the reason because we weren't ready to reveal our own. I fought the urge to remove my shoes and sit with her and ask her what was bothering her. I fought the urge to tell her where I was going. I fought the urge to lie on her lap like I did when I was a kid. I just waved her goodbye and left.

While waiting for my flight at the airport, I remember telling Avni that I was unperturbed by anything. I forgot to add: except a few things, a few people.

CHAPTER FOURTEEN

AVNI

Dad returned in the morning, much earlier than we had expected, and he called it a surprise. Did he believe that we were living a secret life? Was he living a secret life?

The moment he asked mom to iron his clothes, I knew something was off. His tone, his pitch, everything changed when the storm was about to strike. Mom was quiet since morning, as she didn't want to ignite his anger, but his anger was already there, it just needed an outlet. Dad was lying on the sofa, watching television, when mom gave him the perfectly ironed clothes. He inspected his shirt from all the angles, and the fact that it was perfect, pissed him off. He called for breakfast and as mom served him, I knew what would happen next. As expected, he hurled his plate on the floor and used his all-time favorite excuse when he couldn't find any other.

"You want to kill me by adding extra salt?" he yelled, "you know I suffer from high blood pressure."

"I...I am sorry," mom said, her gaze fixed at the parathas and curd splattered all over the floor.

Mom, speak out. The salt was perfect, dad wasn't.

"Bitch!" he lurked over mom and pulled her hair so hard that she lost her balance. Then he pushed her hard and without looking back, picked up his bag from the table and stormed out of the house.

In so many years, I had only heard the sounds and witnessed some slaps, but reality ran deeper than imagination.

"What happened?" Avinash walked down the stairs, but he didn't need an answer. He ran up to mom and when he saw a cut on her forehead, he banged his hand on the wall, not once but many times. Mom was too tired to react, but I held his hand, "Avinash, please stop." I pleaded.

He jerked my hand away, stormed out of the room, returned with a band-aid, and put it on mom's cut. His gaze lingered on her battered face for a while, before he stormed out of the house. Mom gestured me to follow him, so I followed him. As we were leaving, our neighbor came over for her usual gossiping session, no matter how much mom hated it. When she asked mom what happened to her head, mom replied she slipped in the kitchen. Before leaving the house the last words I heard from my neighbor was, "Don't you slip too often when your husband is home?"

Avinash kicked open the gate with a loud bang. He punched everything on his way. He was always the one to comfort me after a mishap, but today comfort seemed far away.

We were already late for our first lecture, so we headed straight to the canteen. Avinash was at the counter ordering coffee when Shreyansh patted me on the back "Hey buddy, so you too got late today?"

This was the last thing I could tolerate that day. He sat too close for comfort and kept his hand on my shoulder. And shocking me, he rubbed his fingers on my neck. Before

I could protest, Avinash's ice-cold tone cut through us, "Shreyansh, remove your hand."

"What?" Shreyansh flinched at his words.

"I said, remove your hand from Avni's shoulder."

Shreyansh immediately removed his hand. "Okay dude, cool. What happened?" He shrugged his shoulder.

"Stay away from my sister." Avinash roared.

"What do you mean?" He shifted away from me in a fraction of a second, stood up, and started rubbing his lips nervously.

"What do you think? I am blind to your inappropriate behavior?" Avinash stood up and walked up to him, his gait aggressive.

"What? Are you crazy? Is this what you think about me?" The way he said that, with hurt etched on his face, I doubted my instincts for a second, but then when I remembered how he brushed his fingers I knew he was just acting

"Your sister is not Aishwarya Rai, OK?" He looked at me with disgust. Damn. I wasn't even a girl, I guess. Why did I think he was making advances? Avinash looked at me and I tried hard to appear unhurt, but that idiotic tear of mine refused to cooperate.

The very next moment, Shreyansh was on the floor and Avinash was on top of him, punching him nonstop.

"Avinash, stop. Please stop it, Avinash." I tried to pull him back, but I stepped back when other boys stepped in to separate them. My trembling hands weren't helpful anyway.

The crowd finally succeeded in separating Avinash and Shreyansh. The first few buttons of Avinash's shirt were broken, but when I looked at Shreyansh, a sinking feeling of dread swallowed me. His spotless skin wasn't spotless anymore due to those red and blue bruises.

I looked at Avinash and my stomach churned. The look in his eyes reflected someone I knew only too well. He could have warned Shreyansh, but he lashed out violently.

JUST LIKE DAD.

At that moment, I feared him for the first time in my life.

Don't be like him, Avinash.

Don't be like him.

CHAPTER FIFTEEN

VIVAAN

I was spending a part of the money I had earned for Arjun on this stupid hotel. But what option did I have? And then I spent some more on bribing the attendant to give me her information. I just had her name. Nothing more. The attendant said she had gone out and he would inform me when she was back. It wasn't before night that he took me to the discotheque on the third floor and pointed towards her.

In the glimmering disco lights, I couldn't see her face clearly. Her long hair was swaying over her face as she tapped to the music, just like my paintings. But in my paintings, she was sad and in a lonely place, maybe missing me. Here, she was in a crowd, dancing to the beats and maybe happy.

Happy.

I walked up to her and started moving my legs to the tune, just to blend in with the crowd. I watched her, still unable to see her face, due to the hair swaying over her face, and the disco lights, but I took in her personality. She was tall and slim, wearing a sleeveless full-length black midi, a tattoo imprinted on her arm - A free bird.

What did her freedom mean? Freedom from responsibilities?

Her steps tapped wildly to the music, but as her gaze met mine, she froze. As if a train running at a speed of 1000 kmph suddenly came to halt.

And then I saw her face. She looked so young. Nothing like the mother of a twenty-three-year-old son. I couldn't name the expression etched on her face. Was it shock? Or fear? Or astonishment? Or pain? Or were they all sharing that little space? How did she recognize me? She had never seen me before.

Never?

Except when I was born. When I was tiny and fragile and defenseless. A cold wave swept through me.

I wasn't sure what it was—the loud music or the blinking lights—that gave me a headache. I wasn't used to it. Or was it seeing my birth mother in front of me? I wasn't used to that either.

She mumbled something to the man who was dancing next to her and walked out. I followed her and ran after her. The silence outside was a stark contrast to the noise inside and immediately gave me some relief.

"Excuse me!" I called out in the lobby.

She turned to look at me.

And then our eyes met.

She froze, except for her hands mindlessly working on opening and closing the clutch of her purse.

"Miss Vedika?" my voice sounded different to my own ears.

"Yes?" she whispered. If she were standing a few feet away I wouldn't have heard her, but I could make out her voice was soft, unlike mine.

Up close, the slight crow's feet around her eyes, and her forehead wrinkles were visible, but it couldn't take away any charm from her beautiful face. Her lips were full, unlike mine, and she was fair, unlike me. What did I inherit from her apart from her height?

Eyes. I have inherited my eyes from her—the rare bronze with hues of black.

After a moment of taking in the sight in front of me, I tried to remember what I was supposed to say. I lost my voice and I wasn't sure whether it would even reach her. Why though? She was standing at just an arm's length not on another galaxy, though it sure felt like it.

"I...I am..." Should I say Appu? Vivaan? Did she even name me before giving me up? What do I say? Your son?

"I think I know who you are." Her voice was broken, and she looked like a different person, not like the one who was dancing carefree, the one who looked happy. Here, she resonated more with my paintings. Though I could see her face, her emotions were guarded, masked, again like my paintings. Her voice was still weak but with the exchange of a few words, I found the distance between us lessening.

"You know? You know I am your," I couldn't utter 'son'.

"I mean...I might...I might know...you are," even she couldn't utter 'son'.

The silence was loaded, the kind that could deafen you.

"I grew up in the Aashiyana orphanage." That was the only thing I could think of to break the stretched-out silence. The weak sentence was again followed by a hollow silence.

She took a step towards me, her hands stretched out, and I closed my eyes preparing myself for the moment, but her hands never reached me.

"I am sorry," she said, and I snapped open my eyes. She had stepped back, her finger again fumbling with the clutch.

Sorry? For leaving me? But before I could delve deeper into my theories, she said, "My husband is coming." She pointed at the glass lifts. "I can't talk to you right now, but can you meet me at 9 a.m. tomorrow at the cafeteria?"

I nodded and before I could say anything more, she walked away.

I stood there, still unsure which way to go, and saw the man catching up with her.

"Who was that boy you were talking to?" asked her husband.

"Oh nobody, just came to give me the purse that I had dropped at the lobby."

Nobody. The word hardly brushed my ears but it blew me off. I just wanted to leave that damn hotel at that very moment, but I somehow managed to drag myself to my room. Maybe masking my emotions so well was a quality that I inherited from her.

A long night before I could meet her again. The whole meeting replayed in my mind. It sounded surreal to me. I had expected so much more from that moment; not a fraction of it was met.

The phone ring pierced the silence that was enveloping me. Mom's name flashed on my mobile but I put it on silent mode. She called again but I still hadn't gathered the courage to take the call. I knew she must be worried, so I made a mental note to call her as soon as I was able to clear up my mind. As if it was going to be anytime soon!

After the longest night of my life, I walked to the cafeteria. I waited till 9.30 a.m. but maybe, she wasn't as keen on our meeting as me, so I got up to leave.

"Wait, Munna..." she said and as I turned back, I found her hand stretched out.

Munna... was it what she named me?

Munna ... I liked the sound of it. Coming from her it sounded like music. Hell, it shouldn't have.

"Sorry, I am late. My husband had a business call at nine but it got postponed to 9.30," she said as she took the chair across the table. She seemed better composed than the first time I had met her. Maybe she was prepared for this meeting now.

"It's ok," I said, pulling my chair.

We both were looking everywhere except at each other. Then there was a lingering silence, an uncomfortable one.

Thankfully, she broke it.

"I know you have questions. And it is natural. But there are things a mother should never say to her son." She swallowed.

My heartbeats stopped at her words. I waited for her to explain.

"I know that you want to know." She started fidgeting with the clutch of her purse again, "know about me, about why I...err...made a decision that...I mean...that separated us." She was choosing her words carefully.

I did want to know but I wanted something more. Maybe a hug, or a kiss on the forehead, or maybe both, or maybe a little bit more. Yeah, it might be awkward, but a moment of reunion between a mother and son should never be awkward for long.

She took out a letter from her purse and her hands reached for mine.

"Read it when you are alone."

As I reached for the letter, my fingers brushed against her hand but I didn't feel any connection. I kept it there a little longer and she didn't pull back. I wanted to feel something. Anything. How was it possible that her touch didn't make me flinch, make me connected to her? Or maybe it did, so intensely that I couldn't feel it.

Her voice pierced my thoughts again.

"I have faced a lot of difficulties in my life. It's just been two years since I got married. I have a family and I can't...I can't keep any connection with you." Her tone was distant, devoid of any emotion but her eyes told a different story.

"I understand." Hell. I didn't understand. I too had a family by God's grace, and I put it all at risk to meet her.

She got up to leave, her eyes refusing to leave my face, but I diverted my gaze towards the letter in my hand. I couldn't gather the courage to watch her leave.

She turned around but she didn't walk away. After standing still for a moment, she turned back.

"I can see you are doing good in your life. And I am happy to know that."

I looked up. I was glad she said that. These were the only words I would like to remember of this bizarre meeting.

"Yeah. Thank you." I somehow managed to say. "Don't you even want to know my name?"

A glint of a tear shone in her eyes. Or did I imagine it?

"No," she paused, maybe to get a grip on her emotions. "For me, you will always be my Munna."

"The small, helpless child you gave away?" I lost it. I didn't want to go there but I just couldn't control myself. For the first time in a decade, I lost control over my emotions, but my voice wasn't loud, it was pathetically weak.

"I am sorry!" Her voice gave away her emotions too and I liked it. That hint of guilt in her voice, a shadow of the pain I had lived in, just a glint of it. But it made me feel I existed. I did matter. Giving me away did matter.

She stormed out as if my presence was suffocating her and this realization suffocated me. Her hands wiping her tears couldn't bring me solace, neither could her unstable steps dragging her. She looked back once from the exit of the cafeteria, and her image blurred behind my tears.

And then she was gone.

I couldn't budge from my place for a long time, my eyes still fixed at the empty exit. I waited for a lifetime for these few moments, the moments that left me feeling more incomplete than I ever did. The letter had crumpled in my fist and before I would ruin it, I dragged myself back to my room. I slumped on the edge of my bed, hunched over the letter in my hand, the weight of it heavy on my heart. Fidgeting with the letter, I stared at it, unsure if I wanted to read it. But that was my only chance so with unsteady hands I unfolded the letter.

Munna,

I don't know where to start. It's been twenty-three years. Twenty-three years is a long time, isn't it? To forgive and forget. And to move on. You must be wondering how one can forget one's child. No, I am not talking about you. You were with me forever. I never tried to forget you or to forgive myself, but I wanted to forget a lot of things in my life and it wasn't possible with you.

There are certain things a mother should never have to say to her son. But it's your right to know the truth.

I was only fifteen. Innocent and naïve, though now those words sound alien to me. I was not in love and what happened to me was without my consent. I don't want to use that dreadful word here. I told you, a mother should not say certain things to her son. When I got to know about my pregnancy, it was late. It was complicated. Abortion could cost me my life.

Not that I cared, but my parents did.

By the time you came, I had lost it all—the innocence, the kindness and even the desire to live. I had never thought I could love you but as hollow as it may sound, in the few moments we were together and in those long years of separation, I have never loved anyone as much as I loved you.

There was nothing I could give you, neither a dignified life nor the happy environment a kid needs to grow up in. Had you lived with me, you would have wondered what a life without me would have been like. Giving you up was the toughest decision of my life, but I never regretted it. Because whatever life you might have lived must be better than what I could have given you.

I can see you have been raised well. Life has been fair to you, more than what I could ever have been to you. With me, you would just be a constant reminder of the place from which you came. A dark sinister place. But you are much more than that. I can see it in you—the kindness. Nothing like the man who is the reason for your existence. I am sure you don't want to know about him.

No matter how much I miss you, I can't keep any contact with you. After a very long time, I am at a happy place in my life.

Not sure how to sign off. I can't say I am your mother and I can't say I am not your mother.

My blessings will stay with you forever.

It was all blank for a while, no colors, no feelings, no pain, no heartbeats. I was cut off from reality, from my surrounding, from emotions and hopes, and expectations. There was just a vacuum and more vacuum.

And then suddenly the vacuum shifted, and reality hit me like a bolt of lightning.

With me, you would just be a constant reminder of the place from which you came. A dark sinister place.

What did my existence mean? How was I ever going to be free from those words?

An elusive feeling washed over me, like a ship being loosened from the anchor and it was about to get lost in the wide ocean. There wasn't any chance of ever hitting the shore again. Where was I supposed to go from there? The darkness that I garnered in the search for light was scary. I hadn't been able to connect with people most of my life and I always thought I might find myself the day I'll meet my mother, but after meeting her I lost whatever was left of me.

'Life has been fair to you,' she wrote. How could she even think that? What the hell did she know of my struggles and my hardships? I just wanted to get the hell out of there as soon as possible. I wanted that moment to wade away in the timeless boundaries of the universe, so far that I could think it never happened.

The letter was wet in my hands now, so I hit the down arrow in the AC almost eight times, but the chill in the room failed to calm my nerves.

My phone beeped and I lurked at it, wanting to distract my thoughts.

"If you feel hungry at an odd time, I have put some dry fruits in the side pocket of your bag." It was a message from mom.

I cried, clutching the phone tight to my heart, and wondering, why did I never paint her?

CHAPTER SIXTEEN

NOEL

Every two years I visited Aashiyana orphanage, the place that gifted me my life; Nidhi and Vivaan. I owed a lot to that place; the donation I gave could never free me of the debt.

Last month when I visited, Simin was sitting on a bench near the park. I closed her eyes with my hands from behind the bench.

"Noel," her voice was shaky, full of emotions.

"That's not fair. How do you always recognize me?" I said, moving to the front and sitting next to her.

"Just like a mother recognizes her son," she said and hugged me. "I thought you forgot this old woman." Her embrace filled me with warmth but I couldn't help feeling sad at how her arms were getting weaker every time I met her.

"You are not taking good care of yourself," I complained.

"Hey, I am fit and fine. Don't you dare make me feel old," she said in the same authoritative tone I always admired. I laughed at that and we chatted for a long time. There were times she floundered with words and I thought she wanted to convey something but couldn't.

"What is it that you want to share?" I asked after a while, taking her wrinkled hand in mine.

"How do you always read my mind?"

"Learned it from you, I guess."

She smiled but her smile withered soon. "Noel, I got a call from Vivaan's birth mother." My grip loosened on her hand but thankfully, I was quick to tighten it again.

"How do you know she was his mother? I remember he was given away without any documentation."

"Who is a mother? Where is my mother?"Six-year-old Appu's voice rang in my mind.

"She was asking about the baby who was left at the gates of Aashiyana on the day we found Vivaan."

Why was his past knocking now when he was finally stable?

"And then?" I asked.

"She disconnected the phone."

"What? Seriously?"

"Yeah, and she never called back."

A wave of relief swept over me and I let out a sigh.

"That's fine, but thanks for sharing it with me. It's fine if it's only her."

"Actually..." she stopped, but that one word was enough to question my belief that Vivaan was finally stable. I took a deep breath, preparing myself for her next words.

"Sometime back Vivaan had called me, and he asked about his birth mother."

Her words pushed me back to the initial days of his adoption. He would wake up at midnight shouting, "Don't leave me ma. Don't leave me." Nidhi used to hug him tight in those moments, fully aware he was not looking for her. She would keep his head on her lap, sing lullabies, and ruffle his hair until he was asleep. I still remember how Nidhi always chose the lullabies of lord Krishna and Yashoda, the perfect mother-son pair who weren't connected by blood. He would dig into her lap crying himself to sleep and only after he slept, Nidhi allowed her tears to flow.

"What did you tell Vivaan?"

"That I didn't know anything about her. And it was not a lie. She had disconnected the phone before I could reply."

"Can I get her phone number?" I asked.

"You want to talk to her?" she stared at me, wide-eyed.

"No," I told her my plan. She wasn't convinced, but for once in my life, I had to disappoint her.

Given the contacts I had, it wasn't difficult to trace her from the phone number. After getting her name and address, I hired a private detective to get some more information. She lived in the US and visited India with her husband only during his business tours.

I passed on the information to Simin and told her to pass it on to Vivaan. He had the right to get his answers. It was a while before we could get hold of her and finally, Vivaan was off to see her.

"Are you crazy, Noel?" This was Nidhi's first reaction when I discussed it with her two days ago. I should have informed her earlier but I couldn't, knowing how much truth would tear her apart.

"Nidhi, of all the people in the world, we should be able to understand him. How can you forget what we did in our quest for truth? Some closures are necessary to move ahead in life." I had said.

"We failed to become good parents." She kept patting Kanha's stomach though he had already slept. "What if she wants him back?"

"Trust your son, Nidhi."

"Trust?" her voice faltered. "Yeah, trust." She had leaned back tiredly on the headrest of the bed.

"Nidhi, believe me, he won't leave us ever. He just wants closure. Who doesn't'? And even if she wants to keep any connection with him, I don't see any harm in it."

"Noel, please." She wanted to say something more but the lump in her throat stopped her. I hugged her and stroked her hair for long until I slept, but I guess she hardly slept that night. After Vivaan left home, she cried for hours. I told her not to disturb Vivaan for a day, but she still called him to check if he was fine. I couldn't blame her.

And now, she was just pacing in the living room, waiting for his return. "Nidhi, please eat something. You didn't have anything apart from tea." I told her, but she ignored me and leaped at the door as soon as the doorbell rang.

I noticed her body tightening as she opened the door, stared at Vivaan, paused, and then hugged him as if she wasn't expecting him to return.

Vivaan's hand came around her after a while "What happened, mom?"

"Nothing! I missed you."

"It's been just a day." His voice was hoarse.

"A long one. Some days start but never seem to end. It was one such day without you."

He closed his eyes. "Yes, it was a long day," he said and pulled back from Nidhi's embrace. When he opened his eyes, I didn't find the relief I was expecting. He forced a smile and walked away to his room without saying a word.

"I told you, she wants him back," Nidhi screamed at me.

"Nidhi, can't you see? She doesn't want him."

CHAPTER SEVENTEEN

VIVAAN

For the first time in many years, I just wanted to stay where I was—in an emotional mess. Even the thought of coming out of it was too much struggle. Mom called me for dinner but I refused, though I wasn't sure if I refused because I wasn't hungry or because I wasn't ready to face them yet. I glanced at the wall clock. 9.00 p.m.

I walked to my studio, pulled out a canvas, and filled my palettes with some random colors, but I couldn't pick up the brush. I kept staring at the empty canvas. How many times I wished I knew which shade to mix for her eyes, which color for her skin, what shape for her jaws? After drawing countless paintings without seeing her, I failed to make a single painting of hers after seeing her. The feeling tore me apart. I tore the canvas, though at the back of my mind I knew every single penny counted and I shouldn't be wasting my canvases, but for once in my life, I didn't care. I didn't care when I threw the brush and palette on the floor. I stormed to the storeroom and pulled out all the paintings and threw them in the middle of the studio.

'*A dark sinister place.*'

'I can't keep any contact with you. I am at a happy place.'
WITHOUT. ME.

I lighted a matchstick and threw it on the paintings, and the hope that I could ever feel complete again went up in flames. My favorite painting where her face was covered as she kissed the child she carried, smiled at me before the fire claimed the last piece of her. Last piece of me.

How wrong I was when I thought I could feel no more pain! The pain that shot through me at that moment was so intense that it became crippling. I wasn't sure how long I stood there with my eyes closed and my fist on my chest, but when I opened my eyes, I saw a hope of healing at the other end of the flames.

Avni.

Healing? Why did I think of that word?

Her eyes went wide in shock, maybe remembering my words, 'Nothing affects me much.'

She walked towards me; the shock obvious on her face.

"Vivaan," she said as searched my face. "Are you ok?"

"No, I am not," I said truthfully, hating the quiver in my voice.

"You burnt the paintings?" She didn't add any more, but her eyes did—you burnt something to ashes, something you couldn't even bear to sell.

I stared at the paintings burning up in flames. A part of me was screaming to put the fire out, another was too impatient to wait for it all to turn into ashes. Avni touched my shoulder and her touch was cathartic. I grabbed her hand and hugged it tightly to my chest.

"I am not ok, Avni. I am not ok." I hated the quiver in my voice, the dampness of my hands, and more than anything, the two people burning down to ashes in front of me.

Before she could say something, I pulled her into a tight embrace. Her hand dangled on either side of me but only for a moment. She wrapped them around me and I dug deeper into her soft neck for some strength. Her earthy aroma awoke my senses and her warmth gave me the comfort I needed. She softly stroked my back. "What happened, Vivaan?"

I didn't reply. I just stood like that for a moment, while she put back some life into me. Then I pulled back and reluctantly sat down on the floor.

"What happened, Vivaan? You can tell me." She sat down beside me.

"She doesn't want me." I pointed to the rising flames. Avni's face reflected confusion, worry, and hurt.

"She isn't who you think she is." It wasn't difficult to read her mind. She was always transparent. "She is my mother."

"Your mother?" She titled her head, her eyes wide.

"Mother … yes." For a moment, I couldn't see the flames or Avni, all I could see was her, sitting at an arm's length, but nothing was ever as unreachable as her. "My birth mother." Her face was still flashing across my eyes. "Who is happy...without me."

And it was then the image melted. I had forgotten that Avni was with me; maybe I was speaking to myself or to the mother who never cared for me. I stared back at the flames.

"There are still people who seek their happiness in you," Avni said softly. Her voice didn't reflect curiosity as if she wanted to know everything in a moment. It intended to give me strength and remind me of my parents.

"Yes, I have the best parents in the world. They adopted me despite my leg—" my voice was cut off when a huge flame claimed my cotton T-shirt and caught fire. I hastily pulled it off and put off the fire. When I turned back towards Avni, her gaze was traveling around my chest. The way she looked at me was...different. Then it dawned on me—she was dressed differently. Her dark eyes were accentuated with kohl, pearl earrings dangled down her ears and touched the thin velvety strap on her shoulders. Her slender arms rested on her thighs where her fingers twitched nervously. Her curvy body looked delectable in a simple yellow midi. And when my gaze traveled back to her eyes, I found a deep affection hiding behind a layer of moisture. Why did my pain affect her so much? She had taken my words seriously about dressing the way she wanted. In the reflection of the flames, she looked radiant, beautiful.

Irresistible.

"In spite of..." She started to say something but stopped.

Her words took me off guard. "In spite of what?" I asked. What was she talking about?

"You were saying your parents..." her voice wavered as her eyes wandered around my chest. "Adopted you." I should have stopped staring at her when she stared into my eyes, but I couldn't. "In spite of..." Her words turned to a whisper before merging into silence.

The flames danced with a rhythm and I gave in.

All I could hear was my heavy breathing. Or was it hers? Or was it our breaths combined as we leaned in and our lips touched, then brushed, and then tasted each other? Her soft lips tasted like fresh dew, and I urged for more. My hand reached her hair, and her fingers dancing on my back sent a fire coursing through me. Hungry for more, I pulled her closer and our bodies flushed together. My mind was diverted from being in a lonely place for too long. From the place, I lost my innocence and a part of me.

A part of me ...I was incomplete... I wasn't supposed to love. I pulled back with a jolt. "I am sorry, I am so sorry."

I got up with a jolt and stormed away, the fire in my veins scaring me. I couldn't be so close to her without kissing her, without loving her in a way I had never loved anyone.

When the silence turned suffocating and she hadn't yet replied, I looked back. She was rocking back and forth involuntarily as if she was trying to come out of the shock of what just happened. Then she got still, just like a painting; the only thing not frozen were her tears. I wanted to comfort her by taking her in my arms, just like she had comforted me a while back, but instead, I said, "I shouldn't have. This was wrong. I. am sorry." I ran my hands through my hair and walked a few steps away. I turned my back to her once again before my emotions consumed me before I could lose control and pull her up for another passionate kiss.

CHAPTER EIGHTEEN

AVNI

He wasn't even looking at me. That just meant one thing. I should have left by now. I wanted to, but my body had jammed to the spot, his touch still coursing through my body. I forced myself to action and got up to leave. Some insane part of me still hoped he would stop me, but he didn't. I walked out silently and then I started running, but I didn't know when I wasn't even walking. When did I stop, when the tears started flowing?

What hurt me wasn't the fact that he regretted the kiss. It was the fact that I still couldn't regret it.

With his touch, something flipped open inside me. As if a box of emotions was locked inside me until now and his kiss was the key that opened that box. I was never going to be the same, I was altered for life.

And. I. Didn't. Regret. It.

The phone beep ignited a small hope—it might be a call from him, maybe he wanted to say that he felt the same. But my heart sank when the name flashing on the phone was 'Mom'.

"I am reaching in two minutes, mom." I disconnected without hearing her reply.

Mom was fuming when I reached home, but when she scolded me, I didn't say anything. I deserved it. Not because I was late, but because of the reason I was late. I just listened to whatever she had to say without looking into her eyes, but sadly enough, her reprimand couldn't divert my mind. Though Avinash was watching the television, I could feel his gaze on me. But I avoided looking at him and walked straight to my room once mom was done.

I stared at the mirror for a long time. I still looked the same, of course. What I was expecting? What changed was on the inside not outside. My hands ran through my hair, wondering if long hair would suit me. My fingers then lingered over my lips, softly caressing the spot through which I connected to Vivaan in a way I never connected to anyone and would probably never will. This shouldn't have hurt as much as it did.

I forced my mind to focus on something meaningful.

Or drift away from something I thought was meaningful.

After changing, I tried to work on the assignment I needed to submit the next day. After almost half an hour, I heard footsteps behind me.

"What happened, Avni? You look upset." Avinash was standing behind my chair, most probably glancing at the blank page on my notebook.

"Nothing. I am fine." I tried but couldn't add any life to that statement.

"You are behaving strangely since some days." He walked to the side of my table, trying to read me.

"Some days? Why don't you tell me exactly how many days?" I looked up.

"What do you mean?" he stepped back, surprised by the sudden change in my tone.

I needed to divert the topic, but there was also something apart from Vivaan that was bothering me for a long time.

"Since the day you beat up Shreyansh." I placed the pen on the book and stood up, my eyes challenging him to accept it.

"He deserved it. He was behaving inappropriately."

"You could have discussed it."

"Avni, I..."

"Wait, Avinash" I gestured him to stop. "I am not done yet. You could have discussed it, but you didn't. It wasn't your anger on Shreyansh alone, it was your anger on dad. We always say to each other 'don't be like her, don't be like him. But in the end, we *are* like them. You vent your anger at the wrong place and I vent out my love at—"

I bit my lips, forcing myself to stop, and turned around, picked up my pen. What for, I didn't know. Maybe I just needed something to hold on to.

"Your love?" He gasped.

"I mean...it's just..." And I suddenly didn't know what to say. I drew some useless lines on the rough paper lying on the table. "I didn't—"

"Tell me, Avni. What is it?" He held me by my shoulder and turned me towards him so that he could see my face. "And how come I have no idea about it?"

"I went with the flow. This isn't what I meant." My voice had mellowed down. I looked up but still couldn't see him in the eyes.

"You know you can't lie to me."

Damn. I knew that.

"Did anyone hurt you?" The grip of his hands on my shoulders tightened, anger seeping through them.

"No," I tried again, faking some confidence in my lie. "No, Avinash, nobody hurt me. Believe me." I still couldn't look him in the eyes as I eased out of his grip. Before I could turn my back to him again, he spoke in such an ice-cold tone that my stomach flipped.

"Look at me."

The way he resembled dad at that moment, the earth slipped from beneath my feet.

"I am fine, Avinash. Just worried about you being angry all the time." I tried to keep my tone even, and before he could say anything else, I added, "I need to finish this assignment. You don't want me to get a bad grade, right?"

"You write the theory part and I will draw the projections for you," he said, still eyeing me sternly as if my silence would reveal something my words didn't.

He helped me with my assignments as usual and around midnight when he finished it, he wished me goodnight and walked to his room.

Next day at college, I couldn't focus much on anything. The last night replayed in my mind endlessly. Shreyansh hadn't been hanging with us since that infamous day and Avinash was talking with his newfound friends but as hard as I tried, I failed to gel with them.

Faking a smile now and then was tiring. And with so much going on in my mind, I just wanted some space to breathe. I lied to Avinash that I was going to the library, but instead, I went to the empty classroom that had been my secret companion every time my mind was messed up.

My phone beeped and to my amusement, Vivaan's name flashed on the screen. Contemplating my options on whether to pick the call or not, I stared out of the window where two love birds were cuddling, unaware of the world around them.

But they didn't look sad.

My gaze traveled back to the phone and I picked up the call, but before I could reply, Shreyansh's voice alarmed me.

"Room no. 15. What's so special about this room, Avni, that you keep walking into this room?"

"Shreyansh!" My tone was sharp, loaded with shock and anger. The way he just spoke, I was sure it was not a normal greeting. There was something in his eyes that unnerved me and my heartbeat quickened as he approached me. The way he looked at me made me uncomfortable. My hands reached my neck, pulling up my T-shirt that was already in place.

"Avni, we are friends. Then why?" Now there was just a bench separating us. I didn't get up from my seat.

"Shreyansh, I am in no mood to talk. Please leave."

"You created a rift between me and Avinash." He pointed a finger at me.

"He said the right thing but in a wrong way," I said, confidently. It wasn't my fault, after all.

"He said the right thing?" There was a pained expression on his face, but before I could doubt my instincts, he added, "well then, so be it. But don't lie that you didn't like it!" He smiled villainously.

"Shreyansh!" I drew in a sharp breath, got up, and walked past him, but he suddenly grabbed my arm and forced me to look at him.

"What do you think of yourself?" his gaze narrowed at me and my stomach clenched. This was not the Shreyansh I knew.

"You are hurting me, Shreyansh." I tried to release his grip with my free hand, but I couldn't even budge a single finger of his.

"Leave her alone right now." A voice roared across the room and I didn't need to turn back to know who it was. I could recognize that voice anywhere in the world. And did I say I loved the anger in his voice? How did he know I was here? Oh, I had picked up his phone, and Shreyansh talked about room no. 15.

"Who are you?" Shreyansh asked, his hand still holding me.

"I said, leave her alone." Vivaan's voice was so cold that it sent shivers down my spine. When I turned around to face him, his burning gaze was fixed at the spot Shreyansh's hand was touching mine, hiding jealousy and protectiveness under the layer of rage.

Shreyansh instantly left my hand and walked towards Vivaan, recognition seeping into his eyes. "Hey, if I am not wrong you are Vivaan, the painter who comes to my dad for his leg job." Shreyansh turned to me next. "What do you know about him?"

The way Shreyansh asked me that, my mouth went dry. I knew by the look in his eyes that there was something about Vivaan I didn't know yet but Shreyansh did and it wasn't pleasant.

I rubbed my arms that were now out of his grip. "You don't need to know what I know about Vivaan." Thankfully, for once in my life, I didn't let my emotions reflect in my voice. I could feign confidence.

Shreyansh ignored me and turned to Vivaan. "When was the last you came to my dad for your leg job?" he looked at Vivaan as if he was beneath him. I felt angrier than I was when Shreyansh had held my hand. I wanted Vivaan to punch him for the way he was treating him, but Vivaan was silent, his expressions unreadable. "I hope you are not thinking of protecting Avni, right? I just need to kick your..." Shreyansh looked at Vivaan's leg and grimaced. "Well, you know." He raised both his hands in the air. "And you will have to spend an hour fixing it." His laugh was pathetic as he looked at me with disgust. "Well, you will make a good pair with this cripple." He pointed at Vivaan and left.

Cripple. The word dangled in the space between us. What was Shreyansh talking about? Shreyansh's dad was an orthopedic doctor and he talked something about a leg job. My gaze traveled to Vivaan's long legs. He was wearing denim jeans and black shoes. There was nothing wrong, but whenmy gaze traveled back to his face, it was written all over his face.

There was a silence, the loaded kind, the suffocating kind. The deafening kind.

Vivaan never lost his guard in so long, but for the second time since our last meeting, I saw the pain etched so deeply in the lines on his forehead, the crinkles around his eyes, the fist around his sides, on his whole body, that it radiated through his body to mine and I felt like crying without even knowing the reason.

"He is right, Avni," Vivaan said after what felt like an eternity, his voice so weak that it hardly reached me. "This is a part of my life and I am used to it." Was that why he was suddenly guilty after that kiss?

"What happened, Vivaan? You care to tell me?"

He turned around to leave without answering me.

"If you didn't want to talk, then why did you call me?" I walked in front of him and raised my mobile to his eye level.

"To say sorry." He stared at my mobile, probably to avoid looking at me.

"For what?"

"For what happened yesterday." His gaze was stubbornly fixed on my mobile as I pulled my hand down.

"A lot happened yesterday. You are sorry for which part exactly? For loving me…" I inhaled deeply. "Or leaving me?"

"For both." He finally looked into my eyes and then he couldn't look away.

"I thought you weren't escapist, but I was wrong."

"I am not trying to escape, Avni. It's just…"

I waited for him to complete the sentence but when he didn't, I asked, "What's stopping you?"

He turned his back to me so I couldn't read him. His guards weren't as strong as they used to be. Was it why he was avoiding me?

"I am not leaving unless you tell me." I declared.

It was quiet for so long that I thought he wouldn't speak, but before I could ask him again, he started, "you remember the video you showed me on your mobile?" His back was still towards me with his hands in his pocket. His frame had hunched a little. Just a little.

I thought for a moment which video he was talking about.

"The one where a child was kidnapped?" He reminded me.

"Yeah," I nodded, remembering the video.

Vivaan walked to the bench, sat on it as if he was suddenly drained. His guards broke down completely. He was no more the stoic person I knew; he was tired of fighting. I tried hard to remember the video and every scene flashed in front of my eyes. The scary void in the eyes of that kid…the void that shook me more than his words. The scene that failed to get any reaction from Vivaan.

Or did I fail to see it? I know that void. I have seen it somewhere. Could it be—? NO, NO, NO!

"It's my story too." The calm in his voice was the shield his eyes failed to provide. Maybe that's why he closed them. But that calm just bared his soul. His pain was so naked, so potent in that moment that he seemed not made of flesh and blood, but of pain. Pain radiated through every particle of his being. The words of the journalist rang in my mind: 'He will never be the same again.'

I swallowed hard, not sure how was I even standing. "No!" I couldn't make it any more than a whisper when I shook my head. It was the worst word I could have uttered.

The boy running behind a bus, a broken heart-shaped pendant hanging from the chain on his neck. It wasn't the pendant, it was his real heart!

"Yes." He finally opened his eyes and my legs gave away. The look in his eyes terrified me. The void there was so intense, so profound, so deep that I couldn't look into them anymore. I glared at the ground, trying not to cry. His voice was emotionless when he spoke again. "Only three things were different from the kid in the video. The first is, I wasn't kidnapped from my home." He paused. Swallowed. "I never had a home. I was taken from an orphanage."

The broken toy home hidden under a pile of toys - It was not a toy home.

I wanted to soothe him, hug him, but I couldn't move. Just couldn't move. He gripped the back of his neck and let out a steady breath trying to stay calm, but his body was giving up. When he spoke again, his voice was detached yet somehow full of emotions. "Second, I returned to the orphanage after being rescued, though not in the embrace of the mother who gave me birth. I was soon adopted by the best mother in the world though."

The woman looking in the mirror was not the one who was staring back from the mirror. One was his birth mother; the other was the one who adopted him.

"And third, they didn't mutilate my hand. They—" He wasn't choking up but he paused, took a deep breath, and swallowed, his fist tight on the top of the bench. "My left leg is a prosthetic one, not real." His voice faltered, and I couldn't decide if that hint of emotion soothed me or broke me into pieces.

The torn book in the pile of books - It was a children's book. It was not just a book, it was his childhood, torn and shattered.

CHAPTER NINETEEN

VIVAAN

The only time pain could be comforting was when it replaced numbness. Just feeling something, anything, gave a sense of being alive. Avni always made me feel something. I couldn't name that feeling, but mostly it was pain because I was constantly fighting my emotions and because that was the only familiar feeling in my life before I gave way to numbness.

And now, once again, I was fighting my desire for her. "I am not the prince charming any girl would dream of," I said, finally, remembering where this conversation was going. She didn't speak and I wasn't sure if it was because she was trying hard not to cry or because she agreed with me. She walked with unsteady steps to the bench on the other side of the aisle and settled on it. It was a while before she said in a shaky voice, "I am not just any girl, Vivaan."

Her words wrapped around me like a blanket in a cold night, but before I could respond she said, unexpectedly, "Want to know my story?"

Her story? I always knew there was something behind her smile, her chatter that sometimes came to sudden halts.

Only now when she wasn't looking at me, did I get a good look at her. Her hands were clutching and unclutching the corner of the bench, her eyes told she had cried herself to sleep last night.

"You know?" The way her eyes were fixed to the ground but not glancing at the floor, she was drifting away to a different world. The way her voice trailed slowly, I knew for sure that, whatever she was about to say she had never spoken before. "I have grown up seeing my mother being beaten like an animal. Dad hits her almost every night he is with us."

I have six months to recoup.

Damn. I should have known.

"I was twelve when mom planned for a divorce and we were happy. *Happy.* As if being happy with a single parent was even possible!" Her mouth twitched as she said this. "Maybe we were just relieved. Then one day..." she paused as a fear grabbed her face. "It was a summer night. The laborers had left for the day. Oh, I forgot to mention. Dad was getting the home renovated, though it was his marriage that needed renovation. When dad realized that mom wanted a divorce, he stormed towards the pile of construction material and picked up an iron rod." She took a deep breath, trying hard to stay calm, "I was horrified...scared...I picked up whatever was handy. It was a stone, a big one." The silence that followed was a long one. When her voice returned, it had changed—it was laden with tremors and insecurity and regret. "I hit my dad's head with as much force as my twelve-year-old self could muster."

Avni involuntarily slid down so she could rest her head on the seat. Each word she spoke, each truth she unveiled, drained her. A defeated look marred her face and she closed her eyes to cut off from the world.

"His back was towards us and he didn't see who hit him. There was so much blood...on the ground, on his clothes, over his face...."

She went still. Then she swallowed a lump in her throat, shook her head, and then again got still. It was long before she started speaking again.

"For a moment I thought I killed him, but thankfully he was still breathing...just unconscious. Mom called an ambulance and meanwhile warned me and Avinash to not utter a word about what happened to anyone. She took the blame and as dad recovered, we knew she could no more file for a divorce. Dad's reports were enough to prove she was dangerous, and that we were not safe with her. And of course, she couldn't leave us with him."

I watched her face while her eyes were closed—she was biting her lips, struggling not to cry, but she was already crying. My willpower was withering and it was getting tougher to maintain the small distance and not gather her up in a hug. But if she knew how much I was hurting to see her in pain, she would know that I cared, so I just sat where I was and watched her shatter into pieces in front of me.

She finally opened her eyes but still didn't look at me. "A daughter should never hate her father, but I do. I hate him, Vivaan. I hate him."

She looked at me finally with regret and hurt and shame. "Since that day, dad's beatings turned ruthless. Mom is punished for no fault of hers. It was my fault, Vivaan. Every time I hear the muffled cries coming from mom's room, I hate myself. I don't know how I face her the next day with the marks she tries to hide! I...I am just so...so...tired." Her voice finally gave way.

With every passing minute I was losing control, to not hold her while she was falling apart was getting tougher. After crying into her palms for a moment, she looked up with tear-stained cheeks. "I am not the shy, obedient girl any man would dream of, Vivaan. I am not the dream girl of any man."

See this sky, subdued in so many colors. The way one nuance envelops the other so that no one can see what's the core of it.

She had told me this for my painting once. At that moment, all the lively, naughty, bold nuances enveloping her core had washed out. And her core scared me because it was so fragile that just a little bit of hurt would break her down. With no control over myself anymore, I got up to cover the one step between us. Her eyes shone with a longing that was hard to ignore, but before I could reach her, a voice roared across the room.

"Avni!"Avinash stood at the door, his eyes bloodshot and his fists tight on either side. Shreyansh stood beside him. Before I could comprehend, Avinash lurked at me and grabbed my collar. "How dare you?" He gritted his teeth.

"Avinash, leave him. Leave him, Avinash." Avni frantically jumped in and pulled his hand away from my collar. Avinash left my collar but continued glaring at me. I challenged his stare but I did nothing I would regret. Avinash stared at Avni, anger oozing through his eyes. "Come with me. Right now." He barked.

"Avinash—" she whispered, almost scared to speak his name.

"Are you coming or not?" He cut through her sentence.

I failed to understand why Avinash couldn't see that Avni was shaking. As much as I wanted to be her shield, I just walked out. Because my presence in her life would bring her nothing more than humiliation and hurt.

The pain of walking away from her was so intense, so profound, so deep, that it reminded me why I chose numbness all those years back.

CHAPTER TWENTY

AVNI

Avinash pushed the door with so much force as we entered our home that my heart cringed. I stood outside for a while, for the momentary tremor to subside before walking in. He avoided me the whole way and since Shreyansh was too keen to listen in to our conversation, I decided it was best to talk after reaching home. Thankfully, mom had gone to the temple and there was no one at home.

Avinash was breathing heavily with his back towards me. I touched his shoulder. "Avinash, it's not what you think. Believe me." I mumbled.

Avinash banged his bag on the couch and everything I had planned to tell him stuck up in my throat. Before I could gather myself, he turned to face me.

"You lied to me, Avni. You lied to me." He pointed a finger at me. "We promised we would never hide anything from each other."

"Avinash!" It took me some effort to face his anger and keep talking. "Listen—"

"There is nothing to listen to." He stormed upstairs.

I stood there for a while to get a grip on my emotions that were bordering on fear. In my nineteen years, I had never been scared of Avinash, and in the last nineteen days, it was the second time he blew me off. I dragged myself upstairs to his room. He was sitting on the edge of his bed, his hands gripped his knees and his gaze was fixed on the floor. I gathered some courage before talking to him again.

"We are not in a relationship, Avinash, we were...are...just good friends." I didn't dare to enter any further inside the room.

"It didn't seem like that, the way you two were looking at each other."

Was it so obvious? I knew about my feelings, but was the affection in his eyes so prominent? I shouldn't have smiled but I did, and I was glad Avinash was still staring at the floor.

"Shreyansh told me that Vivaan is handicapped." Finally, Avinash looked at me.

That word smothered my smile. It took me a while to find my voice, but then I didn't know what to say. I wanted to tell him how Shreyansh misbehaved with me but just at the brush of his finger, Avinash had almost smothered him. If he came to know what Shreyansh did today, he might just kill him.

"Don't say that, Avinash." I fought back my tears.

"Why Avni? Why does that hurt you? You said you were not in a relationship!"

I hated his tone which hinted more at accusation than a question. "We are not in a relationship, but he is a nice person," I whispered, using my words cautiously.

"Last night you said you are venting your love at the wrong place. This is what you meant." It wasn't a question, it was a statement. He got up from the bed, walked towards me, his eyes filled with rage, "What he did to you? Tell me." He held my arms in his both hands. "I will kill that bastard."

"He denied his love for me," I shouted, jerking his hands from my arms. I didn't want to confess that, but Avinash was getting it all wrong. Before he did something stupid like he did with Shreyansh, I had to say the truth.

"So, he has the nerve to reject you. That cripple. Bastard! He has the nerve to reject you?" he shook me.

What did he want? He didn't want us in a relationship, he didn't want him to reject me. What the hell did he want, then?

"He thinks he is not enough for me." I couldn't allow Avinash to misunderstand Vivaan. Avinash took a deep breath, shook his head, and it was a while before he spoke, "Avni, it's not late yet. Just take a step back. It will be difficult in the beginning, but then you will be fine."

I loved the lack of confidence in his voice. "It isn't that easy, Avinash."

"Do you think there is a dearth of complications in our life that you are adding on more?" His voice got louder. His logic was sound but matters of heart never work on logic. Before I could respond, he punched on the bed and stormed out of the room. I stood there dumbfounded, shivering. His anger had spiraled way too much in the last few days.

He returned in about ten minutes and found me sitting on the edge of his bed. His anger had subsided; at least he was pretending he was calm.

"You can't take such important decisions of your life alone. Let me observe him for a few days and if I feel he is right for you, I will support you."

"Oh, Avinash!" I let out a sigh of relief and hugged him. "Thank you. Thank you so much. I knew you will understand me."

"Of course, I understand you. I came in your life long before that cripple."

I pulled back with a jolt.

"Please don't say that, Avinash!" When Shreyansh had used that word, I wanted to slap him. When Avinash said it I was just hurt. I could never hate Avinash. At that moment, I realized our views are so biased with our relationship with the person.

"Ok, I won't say the truth." He said, and I knew it wasn't going to be easy.

Later in the night, recalling the happenings of this odd day, a strange fear of losing Vivaan thudded in my chest. I might have let him believe I was walking out because I wanted to rethink. I didn't even know if he was ready for a relationship.

I was scared it would end when it hadn't even begun.

CHAPTER TWENTY-ONE

VIVAAN

It was time to remove the foreign part of my body with care; my prosthetic leg. I removed it carefully, performed the daily routine of cleaning it properly, and put on the socks on my residual limb. I stared at the missing part for more than I ever cared to. In a very long time, I again wanted to be complete so I could embrace the love I was running away from. I wanted to complain...but to whom? My mother? God? How do you complain to people who didn't exist for you or you didn't exist for them?

Too much delving into the past did that to me. Past crawled up to my present, more profoundly in my dreams. That night I saw him again, the man who took me to that dark room, the anesthesia that filled my nostrils before I gave way...the first moment of realization that I wasn't whole anymore. The raw pain...that moment never left me. The face of that monster blurred but somehow, his voice, chilling to the core, echoed in the space. "That makes you a perfect beggar. A poor handicapped orphan."

I woke up with a jolt, sweating all over. I was not the little helpless boy anymore who couldn't do anything but cry. Years of self-defense training had made me strong enough to keep monsters at bay. Though I had never needed to use my hands on anyone since then. Yes, I wanted to punch Shreyansh in the face when he misbehaved with Avni, but he stepped back just in time. After that, he just showered obscenities at me. Something I could easily deal with. I knew better than to be offended by such meaningless remarks. But Avni shouldn't face all the pain because of me. She deserved happiness, she deserves more than me. I tried not to think about her, but I was thinking about her when I slept when I woke up, and every moment I tried not to think about her.

My feelings for Avni split me into two parts—one desperate to embrace her, the other argued to turn away. The problem was that I didn't know which part was stronger.

When she didn't turn up at my studio the next day, a deep sense of emptiness washed over me. Maybe Avinash was able to put some sense into her. Wasn't that what I wanted?

A week later I was at my studio, trying to focus, but my eyes were drifting to the entrance now and then. Thinking back to a moment with Avni, I picked up my brush and gave into the trance that guided me. Finally, after hours, when I delved out of that trance I was stunned. It was my best painting ever. Avni was sitting on the floor in her yellow midi, her eyes serene yet sad, her pearl earrings dangling over her shoulders. This moment had eluded me since then, the moment before we kissed, the enigmatic pull that was impossible to resist. My thoughts were interrupted by a sound and I turned back.

Avni stood there, her eyes fixed at my leg.

My prosthetic leg.

I was in shorts, intentionally, since the day we last met. Because I wanted her to see the reality if she ever came to the studio. There was a lot of difference between imagination and reality.

"What are you painting today?" She couldn't hide the slight quiver in her voice as she walked towards me.

It's been just a week since I last saw her, though it felt like a decade. More than answering her, I wanted to keep staring at her, memorizing her features, so that I could delve into them in her absence. She looked prettier by the day. Or did my love for her deepen by the day?

"You painted me?" She stared at me wide-eyed.

I didn't even realize I painted you, my hands got out of my control just like my heart. But of course, I wasn't going to admit that.

"It's been a long time since you came for a night walk." I reminded her that she didn't bother to talk to me in a week. And I had to change the topic.

"Dad was home and he doesn't allow night walks." She walked near to the painting, and to me too. She never used to talk about her dad so openly.

"You didn't even call me," I said.

"That tells me that you didn't call me either. Because if you had, you would've known that my phone wasn't working." She gave a sad smile. "But you still waited for my call."

Before I could reply, she surprised me. "You look good in shorts, wear them more often." I knew it took her a lot of effort to say that, and I didn't know if it was because she was a shy girl or if she was hinting that she didn't care my leg was prosthetic.

"It's not a joke, Avni" I tried to avoid being sarcastic.

"You need to tell me that?"

"You don't know what it means to carry this damn thing everywhere." I pointed at my prosthetic leg.

"No, I don't, but I want to know. I want to know about it." She touched my hand. "I want to know about you. Tell me, Vivaan. I am here to listen to you."

I took a moment to think when she said, "Can we sit on the couch and talk? I am really tired today."

It was then that I looked at her face closely. Her eyes were sleepy and her usual charm was missing. I remembered her words: Every time I hear the muffled cries coming from mom's room, I hate myself. It was evident she had hated herself almost the whole week; now she deserved to be loved. At that thought, I immediately shifted my gaze to the floor. I couldn't look at her and not imagine things I shouldn't.

When I didn't reply, she walked to the couch and I followed her. We sat down keeping enough distance. Why the hell did I sit? I could have stood at a distance. How was I going to fight this constant urge to erase the traces of self-hatred emanating from her? There was only one way. Talk about anything... except us.

"It was painful at the beginning. In the growing years, this thing," I pointed at my prosthetic leg, "was impossible to carry. Every time I grew up, it needed a change, and as you can see me," I swayed my right hand up and down my body, "it happened too often. Initially, I couldn't put it on for more than a few hours but as time passed, my body got used to it." I paused, unsure of what to say next. I was never a good talker.

"How old were you?" she asked softly. Generally, I didn't like when people wanted to know about it, because most people asked out of curiosity. But not Avni, she had asked out of concern.

"I guess seven, but I am not sure."

She watched me for a while and then nodded. I never talked aloud about my past to anyone, not even to myself. And the bond I shared with Avni deepened with every word spoken and then, just like that, words came to me without any effort.

"After my adoption, dad organized for a personal tutor since I was not ready to go to school and I had already lost a few years of studies. Mom left her job to be with me in the rough phase of my life." I paused, scared of the words that were ready to leap out from the dark corners of my heart. "But despite all the love from my parents, I missed..." No... I needed to stop there.

I felt Avni's hand over mine when I closed my eyes. I drew in a deep breath. "My mother. I missed my mother." And I didn't know what to say next. I expected Avni to say something—she was the one who always had topics to discuss. But she didn't say anything and we sat in silence for some time. It wasn't an uncomfortable silence. It was the most peaceful silence I had ever experienced in my life. But with this silence, soon I could feel the tension in the air. As if we needed to talk about something else too.

About us. Or about *not us*.

Her eyes were fixed on her painting. "Vivaan?" she said, fidgeting with her fingers. "Our conversation that day... I mean...we... I mean you...I think I..."

"Avni, please stop." I got up from the couch a little too rudely. I didn't dare to look at her face, her eyes that could never hide what they wanted. I couldn't fight back the longing in her eyes, so I turned my back towards her.

"Why Vivaan? Don't you trust me?" She got up too and touched my arm. The slight brush of her hand shouldn't have affected me the way it did. Before I could lose control again, I blurted, "can we just be friends?"

"Ok, but just tell me for once what I see in your eyes is a lie."

I walked a few steps away with my back still at her. It was getting impossible to be so insanely close to her and not love her, not allow our broken pieces to fill in the gaps in each other.

"I am not sure what you see in my eyes."

"Love." Her voice was just a whisper, but it slammed my heart.

"You misunderstood my friendship." I still kept my back on her because I knew.

My eyes wouldn't lie.

CHAPTER TWENTY-TWO

AVNI

Why was he not looking at me? Because I might read him or because he didn't want to see the hurt of rejection in my eyes? Whatever the reason, I was glad he was not looking at me. I utilized the moment to wipe away my tears.

My gaze shifted to the painting. I never knew my eyes were so expressive. How did he paint that longing in my eyes without feeling it? Was it also a nuance of friendship? Or did he lie? Why did he suddenly shift to shorts? To weaken my resolve?

To tell the truth, seeing his prosthetic leg had paralyzed me for a moment, and I was thankful because if I wasn't paralyzed, I would have screamed. It was a metal leg, a thick rod hanging down his knee. It made me feel something for him. No, it wasn't pitying, it was a feeling of helplessness.

I couldn't do a thing to make it better. Nothing.

A choking sensation filled my heart and it was hard to breathe, but thankfully he was so engrossed in painting me that before he turned back, my heart had regained its normal rhythm.

Once I was sure I could speak, I said, "Just friends? okay, no problem. Let's start with friendship." I walked to his front and forwarded my hand for a handshake.

He was unreadable when he hesitantly forwarded his hand. A thousand emotions engulfed me merely at his touch and I wanted to scream: We can never be *just friends*! But I didn't voice my thoughts.

I held on to his big rough hands for a little longer, letting my body feel the connection until he pulled away.

"Well, can we sit on that couch again? I am really tired, but promise I won't take any undue advantage, even though you look so good in shorts."

Shit. Why couldn't I act normally around him? Now having made the blunder, I didn't want to back off.

"Well, you don't feel anything for me, but you can't stop me from feeling. Right?"

He didn't say anything, but I caught his lips curving up the slightest bit as he shook his head, treading towards the couch.

He let me sit first and sat as far as the couch allowed him, but my heart was beating erratically, especially after my stupid comment. With a two-day-old stubble on his face and the obvious tension, he looked so adorable that I had trouble focusing. When our eyes met the tension grew heavy. The passionate kiss we shared the other day lingered in the air between us. My heart would have exploded at the mere memory of the kiss if I didn't start speaking.

"You remember the doll I drew?" I asked, and he nodded. "It was a doll I stole from a shop. But hey, don't judge me. I was just seven and I placed it back in a few days." I was scared of what I would find in his eyes when I looked up, but the way he was smiling, I was sure he wasn't disgusted.

"And do you know my incisor tooth is a false one?" I opened my mouth and touched my tooth. "I fell while playing football when I was thirteen and broke it."

Shit. It was a blunder. A false tooth couldn't be compared to a prosthetic leg.

"Avni, stop being stupid, okay?" he said, but before I could worry that I had offended him, a big smile erupted on his face and then he started laughing.

He laughed!

CHAPTER TWENTY-THREE

VIVAAN

Only Avni could do that—make me laugh amid chaos. She could divert my mind from the worst of emotions.

The mere thought of parting with her someday was scary. I didn't know where our relationship was going, but I just couldn't battle my need for her. Concealing love with friendship wasn't easy, but it was the only way to be together.

I never wore shorts in my whole life since I lost my leg, except in school for a few years where it was the uniform, and a few days back when I tried to show the reality to Avni, but now I wore them to the studio. Not to weaken Avni's resolve anymore though. I was comfortable and didn't need to hide when I was with her.

It was a constant struggle to keep my hands away from her after knowing her feelings. Most of the time they were either folded at my chest or prisoned in my pockets. The weakest moments were when she laughed and her dimples deepened. She looked angelic with her child-like innocence.

But now she didn't come to my studio often as her father was home most of the time. Though we often met at the college canteen. One day, the canteen was full so we walked up to the farther end of the college garden. This unattended part with an unfinished laboratory was discarded years ago when the huge laboratory was built in other part of the college. The structure here only had an unfinished room and a small porch that had two huge pillars holding the broken porch roof.

"This place is so beautiful." Avni said, dusting the porch with her handkerchief, and looking around at the trees shielding the place. "And we also don't need to order something just because we are sitting here." She chuckled, as if it was a relief. Though the grass had gone wild and the porch had layers of dust due to negligence, I loved the peacefulness that was a stark contrast to the noisy canteen where someone was always waiting for us to leave the seat so that they could sit. But the place was secluded and it wasn't a good idea to be there with her. Unaware of my internal turmoil, she cleaned the sat down on the porch and gestured me to sit. I sat down hesitantly, but within no time her nonstop chatter made me comfortable. Mostly, she talked about her childhood memories that revolved around Avinash. In some time she received a call from Avinash, inquiring where she was. Avinash was there within five minutes. The look of disapproval on his face was evident when he reached there and I couldn't blame him.

"Are you crazy? Why are you here? It's risky," he said in an angry tone.

"Risky?" Avni made a face. "It's just the end of the garden. It doesn't even take two minutes to reach the main garden."

"But," he looked around, "it's totally cut off. I didn't even know there was place to sit here." He looked at the porch.

"I was not alone. Vivaan was with me," she said.

I couldn't say if Avni didn't understand that Avinash was hinting she wasn't safe with me or if she was trying to ignore what he meant.

"Vivaan?" Avinash grimaced, staring at my leg.

"Avinash!" Avni retorted before the uncomfortable silence took over.

"I have a class, I need to leave," I said and left. I tried to avoid Avni after that incident but she persistently called me. She also apologized on behalf of Avinash, but frankly, I didn't blame Avinash. Though I tried my best to avoid her, I couldn't fight my urge to see her on the seventh day so I agreed to meet her. The college canteen was full so we walked to the same secluded part of the garden.

"It seems Avinash doesn't like me much," I said, standing with my back resting on a tree trunk, and my hands in my pocket. Avni stood at an arm's length.

"It's not about you Vivaan. He gets too protective for me. We had a troubled childhood. After knowing your sufferings, I feel small saying this to you, but in the little world we lived in, it was traumatic. The shouts, the cries, the beatings...we felt so helpless. Whenever dad hurts mom and mom doesn't respond, Avinash hugs me and tells me not to be like her and I tell him not to be like dad. He worries that someone might hurt me, that's all. It's not about you."

She looked so sad in that moment that I couldn't help it. I just pulled her in my arms and stroked her back. I couldn't let her carry that pain alone, and without a second thought, she wrapped her arms around me. I hoped she couldn't feel my heartbeat that had accelerated at this sudden closeness, but that wasn't possible because this close, I could feel the increased rhythm of her breathing.

"I am tired, Vivaan. I am tired. With dad, his aggressive behavior. He hasn't been on an official tour since long. And...."

Her thoughts drifted away.

"And what, Avni?" I was still stroking her back, conscious of every inch of her body against mine. Every fibre of my body was jolted out of deep sleep. I tried to step back but I couldn't. How could I let her feel that she was alone in this?

"He was always violent but since that incident his beatings have got ruthless."

"I think you should confront him."

"Are you crazy?" she looked up at me, surprise written all over her face.

"What is the point of feeling guilty when you are not working on it?"

"I promised mom!" her grip loosened around me.

"What did you promise, Avni? That you'd let your dad kill her, but you won't utter a word? That you will just stand like a coward in your room, hug your brother and say 'don't be like him?'"

"Vivaan!" she gasped, taking a step back, moving away from my embrace.

"I am sorry, Avni, I didn't mean to hurt you, but I speak my mind. You know that."

"I shouldn't have told you!" she said, hurt evident on her face, and she turned around to leave.

Before I could say anything, I saw Avinash standing at a distance. Avni stopped in her track when she saw him glaring at us.

"What happened? Why are you crying? Did he hit you?" his fist was tight.

When a man beats a woman, he doesn't just damage her, he damages the kids who grow up witnessing it, the people associated with those kids. The man who beats a woman damages the whole next generation. Avinash was a live example. Considering how much he loved Avni, his possessiveness was justified. The slightest frown on her face could rip him apart. Unfortunately, I was different. I believed that sometimes, you need to push people off the edge to liberate them. And under Avinash's caring cocoon, Avni could never feel liberated, never become strong. According to Avinash, just dressing like a boy and behaving like one would make her strong. But who said a man was stronger than a woman? Utter nonsense.

"No Avinash, at least think before you speak." Avni retorted.

"Tell me what happened?" he demanded.

"Nothing. Let's go home." she walked away. Avinash followed her, but not before giving me a warning glare.

CHAPTER TWENTY-FOUR

AVNI

Vivaan's words cut through me. He talked straight to the point of arrogance, but then that's what I loved about him—telling the truth without any sugar-coated words.

Avinash probed me to tell him why I was crying, but I was in no mood to discuss.

Mom was in the kitchen, chopping onions, when we reached home. There wasn't a strand of grey amid her black hair, yet she looked older than her age. Worry was etched on the dark circles beneath her eyes, a constant fear was imbibed in the wrinkles on her forehead. The sleeves of her blouse needed alteration, she had shrunk further in the last month.

The frantic ringing of the doorbell interrupted my thoughts and before I could even blink, mom was at the door.

"Why so much time to open the door?" dad shouted, throwing his mobile on the couch.

I walked out. "she opened the door as fast as she could, dad." The way dad looked at me and then at mom, I couldn't say if he was shocked or furious.

"Is this the way to talk to your father?" He stepped towards me.

My stomach churned at the way he looked at me with his cold hard stare. I inhaled the much-needed air before replying, "I said nothing wrong."

"Go to your room," he said in a steely tone, pointing upstairs, his hands trembling with anger.

I froze to my place, my legs sealed with both, fear and determination.

"Go to your room now," he repeated, his words emotionless, rage emanating from every particle of his existence.

"Go to your room, Avni." Mom's voice trembled. I fought with my impulse to just turn around and run to my room; I stood there, digging deeper for courage.

"So that you can beat up mom?" I wasn't sure, from where I found the courage. Whether it was years of anger that lashed out or my inability to let Vivaan think of me as a coward.

"You bitch!" Dad raised his hand and I closed my eyes, waiting for a deadly bolt to hit me to the ground but it didn't come. Scared to face the truth, I opened my eyes. Dad's hand was in Avinash's strong grip, mid-air.

"Don't you dare hit my sister." Avinash was the mirror image of dad, but in that moment the difference between them dawned on me and filled me with comfort.

Dad used his strength to hurt, Avinash used his to protect.

"Your sister? She is also my daughter!" Dad pulled away his hand from Avinash's grip and stepped back.

"Unfortunately, yes." Avinash pointed at me and then at himself. "Unfortunately, you are her dad and mine." And then he pointed at mom. "And you are her husband. But a husband should be a protector, dad, not a predator." His pitch was high. Avinash had always wanted to rush down when dad hit mom, but I was always scared upon remembering the consequences of the day when I hit dad. I was always worried something of that magnitude might repeat itself but today, seeing me standing in support of mom, Avinash joined me.

"My kids! My kids who I loved more than my life are talking to me like this!" Dad crashed on the sofa dramatically.

"Love? What do you know about love, dad? Stop overacting." Avinash lashed out.

"Oh yeah, I never beat her to death. But you know, you all know." He pointed at mom. "This bloody bitch could have taken my life."

"It was me, dad. I was the one who hit you." My voice barely made it to my own ears; there were other sounds more prominent, like the sound of my heart thumping against my chest, the blood running through my veins, and a screaming silence in some distant corner of my mind. After momentary darkness, I saw the shocked faces around the room. I couldn't say if mom was disappointed in me, or disgusted or worried or if dad was more shocked or hurt or angry. But Avinash's eyes reflected pride. That was the only thing that held me upright in that trying moment.

After sucking in the much-needed oxygen, I pushed out the words. "I just wanted to save mom. You could have killed her that day."

"So, you all want to see me dead." Dad's voice wasn't loud, it was scarily low and it broke me. "You are a load of bastards with whom I wasted my life." He dragged his legs to his room.

As much as I was proud of saving mom, I failed to free myself from the guilt of hitting my dad. That guilt was like a slow poison that was claiming me piece by piece, but saying the words aloud was like spitting a part of that poison out of my system.

"You shouldn't have said it, Avni." Mom said, tired. She didn't even scold me as I had imagined, and it broke my heart. Her voice was weak as if it was taking a huge effort even to speak. I looked at her and then at the photo hanging on the wall behind her—of mom holding me and Avinash when we were kids. Where was that woman lost? The weak, terrified woman standing in front of me wasn't her. She was lost somewhere in saving her family. When it comes to family, the strongest of the women compromise with their honor.

"Don't say anything, mom. You look tired, you need to sleep." I walked to her and held her hand.

Mom looked at the bedroom and her thoughts were evident on her face.

"Mom, please sleep with me today," I said, and Avinash nodded in agreement.

Later in the night, I slept with mom, holding her tight, clinging to her like I did when I was a little girl. Back then, she told me stories of courage and strength, but she wasn't the same woman anymore. She cried but I didn't stop her; I cried but she didn't stop me. Crying was not always bad.

Next morning, dad didn't go to office and it scared us. We knew he was waiting for me and Avinash to leave so he could lash out his revenge. Avinash stayed at home to keep a watch on dad while I attended college.

I had received many messages from Vivaan last night but I couldn't reply. He had written 'sorry' but I guess he didn't need to apologize. His harsh words held truth, but

I liked it that it mattered to him that he had hurt me. He was changing with every passing day, and was opening up with me. Not that he would speak for hours, but he started sharing little tidbits of his life, and it meant a lot.

After college ended, I met him at our favorite spot. He was pacing in the little space when I reached there. As soon as he saw me, he rushed towards me. "Thank God you came. I thought you were mad at me." He ran his fingers through his hair. "You didn't even reply to my messages."

"So, you have started worrying if you hurt me," I mocked him.

"I always did." His face fell. Maybe he did but never expressed it, until now. I wanted to say something but I was feeling so tired after the happenings of the last day that I walked to the nearby tree and took its support.

"What happened, Avni? What's bothering you?" The concern in his eyes just broke me. Why the hell he couldn't accept his feelings?

I told him all that happened last night. "I never wanted to be in a relationship because I was scared that every man was like my father, but when I met you..." I bit my lip, turned halfway towards the tree, and scratched the bark of the tree with one hand. On any other day I would buck up and bear his rejection, but not today.

"What happened when you met me?" His voice held hope, fear, concern and desire. How could a few words carry so many emotions?

"You don't like me talking this way."

"No, it's ok. Tell me whatever you feel. I want to know." He reached me, and stopped my hand from scratching the bark, his other hand holding the tree.

I stared at our hands on the tree. "Vivaan, you know I—"

"There will be no turning back, Avni, so be sure of what you say."

"You still doubt me?" I finally looked at him, deeply hurt.

"I have never trusted anyone the way I trust you." He stepped closer. "You know what? After meeting my mother for the first and the last time, I found myself so cut off from reality that I thought I don't fear anything anymore. But I fear one thing, Avni."

His eyes weren't guarded. They screamed how much he loved me and unguarded Vivaan was so damn irresistible that I couldn't speak or even breathe.

"I fear losing you." There was so much emotion in his voice that my heart leapt out of my chest. "I fear losing you, Avni." He pulled me closer and before I could comprehend, his arms were around me, my face was pressed to his chest. The desperation of his embrace was enough proof of how hard he had restrained himself. I didn't know when I wrapped my arms around him, when my tears started flowing, but I remembered the feel of his erratic heartbeats, the smell of his perfume, the sound of our breathing, and the raw emotion tickling every inch of my body.

Then he stared at me with such ferocity that suddenly my body turned limp in his embrace. His hands cupped my cheeks and his gaze rested on my lips. My hands tightened at his back and I closed my eyes, thrilled, excited, scared all at once in anticipation of what was coming. The warm touch of his soft lips on mine sent tremors through my whole body. What started tenderly soon turned fierce and every fibre of my being was altered by his touch. I knew this moment would forever be engraved on my soul. After a long, passionate kiss, my heart was still beating hard when we separated. Finally, when I opened my eyes, I didn't look at him but I could feel his gaze on me.

He lifted my chin, so my face was towards him, but I averted my gaze. I couldn't look at him.

"Avni, look at me. I want you to remember this moment."

My whole body trembled at the raw emotions in his eyes. That intense stare aroused more reactions in me than the kiss we just shared. The words he spoke next were the most beautiful words I had ever heard in my life.

"I love you."

Those words penetrated inside me, my soul, my blood, my flesh and became an inseparable part of my identity.

CHAPTER TWENTY-FIVE

AVNI

It was a weekend and Avinash was out on some errand. I was thinking about the sapling I had sown with Vivaan and the cozy moments we had shared later when a loud bang startled me. It was followed by a scream. I rushed downstairs and the scene there sucked the air out from my lungs. Mom was lying on the floor, blood oozing from her head. Dad was standing behind her with a strange look in his eyes and a hockey stick in his hand.

He didn't look like my dad at that moment. I had never seen so much hatred in his eyes before, I had never seen so much hatred in anybody's eyes before. And the moment our eyes met, I realized there were now two people in the room with so much hatred.

He tossed the hockey stick on the floor and strode towards me. I held my breath, but he passed by me and stormed to the living room.

I pulled out the first aid box from the cupboard and rushed to mom. She was groaning, curled up on the floor, her hands pressed on the open wound on her forehead. I pulled her head up to my lap, cleaned her wound, and covered it up with a bandage. My hands trembled, and my throat hurt, as I tried hard not to cry. After cleaning her wound, I helped her to her room, made her lie on the bed, and pulled the blanket over her. Then I walked to the living room.

Dad was watching television. Seriously?

I wasn't Avni at that moment. I was anger, rage, and revenge. I dialed the number for Woman Helpline before I could change my mind. My voice was unsteady when I spoke, "We need help, there is a case of domestic violence—"

The next moment I was on the floor, stars dancing around me in absolute darkness. When I got my vision back, dad's cold hard stare froze on me. The first thought that jolted through me wasn't how much it pained. It was; how did mom survive this humiliation for so many years? The tears that followed were not only of physical pain, they were the tears of shame of being born in a family like this, tears of humiliation my mother underwent all her life, and tears of regret at why we didn't stand up for mom earlier.

"Don't you dare!" Dad snorted. I couldn't reply though I wanted to; my head was hurting too much.

He walked away and settled on the couch again, watching the cricket match. It took me some time to get back to my senses and get up. I walked to the kitchen to get a glass of water when the doorbell rang. I was about to walk out of the kitchen when dad entered the kitchen, his face pale.

"You bitch!" He looked like a stranger when he said that. "The police is at the door, don't you dare!" He pointed a finger at me.

I didn't even give them my address, as I just wanted to scare dad. They might have traced the number. But I still didn't regret my decision, because the fear on dad's face made it all worth it.

"Don't *you* dare." I snarled back.

"I will tell them your mother wanted to kill me years back," he whispered as I was about to step out.

"Enough, dad. I will admit that it was my mistake and I will tell them why I did it." I looked him in his eyes before walking out.

There was a lady and a male constable at the door. Mom was also in the living room, unaware of the chaos that had occurred in the few minutes she lay down.

The lady constable's gaze traveled to the bandage on mom's head, then to the lump on my forehead, and then to dad standing frozen at the farthest corner of the room.

"What happened to your head?" the lady constable asked mom.

"I...I slipped in the bathroom." She didn't look up from the floor, embarrassment written all over her face.

"And what happened to your head?" she pointed her finger at my head.

"She slipped from the stairs." This time it was dad. He was so eager to cover up his act, that it became even more evident.

"How come, you all are slipping on the same day?" The lady constable's eyes narrowed at dad for a brief moment, then wandered on all of us. "Someone complained of domestic violence from this address."

"It...it must be a misunderstanding." Mom was still eyeing the floor.

"What do *you* have to say?" The lady constable turned to me.

I was weighing my options when I saw Avinash at the door. His gaze traveled from the lady constable to the male police officer.

To mom...to the bandage on her head.

His eyes flickered. He fisted his hand as his gaze traveled to dad.

Then finally he looked at me...at the lump on my forehead. His jaw tightened and he strode towards the lady constable. "What's going on?"

"Someone called from here, complaining of domestic violence."

I was not alone in this. I knew Avinash would support me.

"What? That's not possible. I am sure you got it all wrong."

No. No. No. Not you, Avinash.

"Doesn't seem so." She pointed her finger at me and then mom. "Sir, please come with us." She turned towards dad.

"You can't take me like this without any warrant." Dad snarled.

"Whose number is this?" She handed a paper to Avinash and he stared at me. "Avni."

"Unless she tells us to leave, we are not leaving." Just the way she stood there, doing nothing except staring at dad, and still making him flinch, was noteworthy. The lady had earned my respect.

Avinash gestured me with his eyes to stop this; he seemed disgusted with me.

"I am sorry for bothering you, ma'am. I don't have any complaint." I said finally, still not convinced. Her eyes rested on my fingers fidgeting senselessly and I willed my hands to stop.

"I can see the circumstances of your denial." She sternly eyed dad, mom, Avinash, and then back at me. "But don't hesitate to ask for help if you ever need it."

It was strange how a smile covered my face amid this chaos.

"Sure," I said and led them to the door. My neighbors were sneaking on us from their windows and whispering amongst themselves.

There was a harrowing silence after they left. Nobody moved. We were still standing at four corners of the room until dad stormed out of the house.

"Are you crazy? All the neighbors were watching." Avinash yelled as soon as dad left, his face filled with shame. "We could have sorted this out." He paused. "I could have sorted this out."

"What happened to you, Avni?" Mom's voice wasn't loud, but it held accusation. "You were a quiet girl." I didn't like the look of shame in her eyes. I couldn't face the accusation in the eyes of the two people who meant the world to me.

"Yes, I was a quiet girl, mom, whom you covered in a boy's clothes just to cover your guilt that you couldn't raise me a brave person." I wanted to stop there, but I couldn't. It wasn't the anger of this day, it was something that had bubbled up over years. "A girl doesn't get bold by dressing like a boy. She becomes bold by standing up for what she believes in and by fighting for her rights. Going against the society if the need arises, not just for some silly comparison of being equal. Do you understand that?" I had lost control of my pitch that was edging on sarcasm. My eyes were stinging with tears I was trying hard to hold back.

"This is not your language," Avinash exploded, "this is the language of that cripple." He pointed vaguely out of the door.

"Cripple? Who cripple?" Mom stepped towards me with a thousand questions in her eyes.

"Avinash, please stop," I warned him.

"That handicap boyfriend of Avni's."

I wanted to slap Avinash for the first time in my life.

"Avni, is he right?" There was suddenly an edge to mom's weak voice as she stepped closer.

"Yes, mom, Avinash is right." I stared at Avinash and then back at mom. "I love that cripple." I also pointed vaguely out of the door. "I love that handicapped man. Because people who are handicapped by the body are better than people who are handicapped by soul. I want to be loved by a cripple rather than being beaten by a macho man every day. Is there anything wrong with it?" I was losing it. My voice was wobbling, but I had to say it. "Yes, I love that cripple. That cripple, that cripple." I kept on repeating the word 'cripple' until I was sure Avinash could never match its magnitude. And then, leaving mom and Avinash staring dumbfounded at me, I stormed to my room with unsteady steps and collapsed on my bed. We didn't discuss anything thereafter—neither about dad, nor Vivaan—and we all drifted to a harrowing silence in our respective rooms.

Dad returned late that night, but apart from anger there were traces of fear on his face and a strange satisfaction filled my heart. He announced dramatically that he couldn't live with rubbish people like us and that he would soon arrange for a long business tour. He stayed true to his word, and left within a week; he didn't tell us for how long. But from his phone conversations, we knew it would be a couple of months at least.

After the long wait when I finally met Vivaan, he pulled me in his embrace. "You ok?"

It was strange how before that hug "yes" as an answer would've been a lie, but now in the shield of his arms, it was the truth.

137

CHAPTER TWENTY-SIX

VIVAAN

She froze at my words. The only thing moving were her tears rolling out from her big brown eyes.

"Sorry for always being a cry baby," she said between sobs.

I hugged her once again. "That only proves you are full of emotions. Just be the way you are. Okay?" At those words, her grip tightened around me and she dug deeper in my chest. That moment was surreal was all I could say.

"Can you also hear this music?" She looked up at me amused as if the music was unreal.

"Of course, Avni, your phone is ringing." I shouldn't have smiled, but she made me smile in the weirdest of moments. She mumbled 'oh shit'before picking up the phone.

"I am coming." She sighed into the phone. "I know I am late. Let me come home and then ask all that you want to. Okay?"

She looked back after putting her phone back in her pocket, her face flustered. "You know Avinash calls me a blunder queen."

"Suits your personality." I teased her "By the way, the music was apt for our situation."

She smiled and suddenly, I started laughing out loud. I didn't remember laughing so hard ever. I felt that laughter in every part of my body.

"Now you are embarrassing me." She hit on my chest with mock anger.

"I am sorry." I pulled her to me again. I couldn't get enough of her. "But you know what? I love your blunders." I whispered in her ears and she gasped at how it made her feel. After hugging each other for a solid minute, her voice turned grim. "I should leave now."

She was upset to face the situation at her home and I was responsible for putting her in that situation, but I didn't regret it. The path to healing passed through pain. She would go through many heart-breaking moments in that phase, but she would come out stronger, bolder and happier.

But still, the sadness on her face broke me. I pressed my lips on her forehead. "You are a strong girl. Never forget that." She nodded, digging her head once again in my chest and I knew she was crying. I just wanted to hold her like that forever, protecting her from what she was to face in the coming days, but I let her go to face her fears.

I stayed there long after she left, reminiscing the best moments of my life; of the feel of her lips against mine, her face against my chest, her imprints in my soul. It became my favorite place on earth, the deserted porch with dense trees surrounding the place, shielding our love from the world.

That night she couldn't visit my studio, but the next day we met at the same place.

"How are things at your home?" I asked her, gesturing for her to sit beside me on the porch. She sat down next to me.

"Tense. Dad went to the office today, but he is still in a horrible mood." She said weakly and rested her head on my shoulder. I wrapped her fingers around mine and pulled our joint hands to my chest.

"You know people carve their names on trees as a semblance of their love?" she said, suddenly changing the topic. I nodded, hoping she wasn't hinting we do that because what I knew of her was that she could never hurt anyone.

"But I believe love shouldn't be destructive. If anything, love should give life not hurt, so I have got something." She drew her hand out of mine and pulled out a small sapling from her bag.

"We will sow this sapling together, and watch it grow with our companionship."

I let out a sigh of relief, wondering how was it that every day I thought I couldn't love her any more than I already did, but the very next day I would prove myself wrong.

The ground was soft with the drizzles of the morning rain and we dug the ground with a pointed stone. Then we both placed the sapling in the mud, our hands touching over each other with every act. There could be something better than a kiss—the way an innocent touch connected you.

Once the sapling was sown, she poured water on it from her bottle. There wasn't much water in her bottle for us to wash our hands, so I picked up dried leaves and wiped my hands on them, but she surprised me by wiping her hands on my T-shirt.

"Hey stop, my mom will kill me." I held her hand but my light blue T-shirt was all brown by then.

"You can't get away with that. Ok?" I had already wiped my hands on the leaves, but a little bit of dirt was still left, and I wiped my hands on her clothes. She tried to get out of my grasp, but I didn't let her go and wiped my hands all over her. Her softness ignited a fire and within seconds we were kissing and hugging, and feeling each other, so fervently that I feared my chest would rip open until she finally pushed me away, gasping for breath.

"If this is how we sow a plant, I want to grow a forest," I said once I had my breathing in control.

"What happened to the gentleman who always had his hands in his pocket or folded around his chest?" she asked, a blush rising on her face.

"You started it," I played innocent. "Every time I look at this little plant I am going to remember how you took advantage of me."

"Shut up, ok?" She fisted on my chest. Then standing side by side, with one hand holding the other's waist, we stared at the sapling in unison. We promised to water the sapling until its roots were deep enough to fend for itself.

CHAPTER TWENTY-SEVEN

VIVAAN

I gathered her in my arms and she snuggled in, holding me tight, digging her face in my chest. I loved it when she did that.

"You are a strong girl." I stroked her back.

"Not everyone thinks that way." Her words were muffled against my T-shirt "I have heard enough in the past week, what a horrible daughter I am, God shouldn't give anyone a daughter like me...even that's why people pray for a boy..." Her voice trailed off by the last word.

"Who said that?" I removed the dried leaf from her hair that had just landed there.

"Neighbours and relatives."

"Those people are foolish."

"Even mom and Avinash?" She bit her lips.

"They told you all that?"

She tried to say something but just shook her head instead. She looked more tired than I ever saw her, so I held her hand and led her to sit on the porch with me. Once we were seated, I resumed the conversation, holding her close by her shoulder. "Stop overthinking. They are also stressed out like you. Give them some time and I am sure they will understand."

She just nodded and plucked a grass blade from the ground, and rolled it around her fingers, staring at it with a faraway look on her face. She was silent and I missed her non-stop chatter.

"I have a surprise for you."

"What? A painting?" Her eyes lighted up, just a little.

"Check it yourself," I said, and gave her the gift.

She opened the pink wrapper and bit her lip when she saw the gift. She traced her fingers over the doll. "The best gift I ever got," she said, trying not to cry.

"Isn't she like you?" I stroked her cheek.

"No. She didn't try to send her dad to jail." And finally, the tears she held for so long rained down her cheeks. "What an awful daughter I am! I was happy to see fear in his eyes...I...I..." She tightly closed her eyes. "What was I trying to do?"

"You didn't harm your dad, Avni, you only protected your mother."

"Why do I always make choices that make me hate myself?" She placed the doll on her lap and sobbed, her palms covering her face.

I had to suppress the urge to love her when she went through the same feelings in my studio. Fortunately, now I could let her know she deserved more love than anybody.

"Sometimes life forces you to take tough decisions. That doesn't make you a bad person. Do you understand that?" I removed her palms from her face, turned her face towards me, cupped her cheeks, and kissed them, tasting her tears. "You couldn't just ignore all you saw without doing anything." I kissed her again, on the spots just next to her eyes. She got still with that touch and her warm hands wrapped around mine. This close, I had trouble focusing on my words. "What you did needed courage, not everyone can be as brave as you," I whispered before kissing her forehead and then her chin. My emotions were going haywire with every new touch and the way her breath hitched, her cheeks turning to new shades of red, I was sure her heart was beating just as fast as mine. We stared at each other in silence for a while until slowly, hesitantly, she moved her hand into my hair and her gaze traveled to my lips. Then she slowly pulled me in for a kiss. The touch of her soft lips created desires anew and we kissed again; once, twice, thrice, until we finally lost count.

Her face was flustered when she pulled back, forcing some distance between us. She stared at the doll, her fingers senselessly fumbling with the border of the doll's frock. Once my heart regained its normal rhythm, I asked, "is this doll like the one you stole from that shop?"

Her lips curved into a smile as she nodded.

"So, you like plump dolls, not lean ones?" I asked.

"Avni doesn't play with dolls!"

We both jerked at that voice. We didn't need to turn back to know the owner of the voice. Avinash! Damn. When did he come? I guess, I hope, just now.

"What do you mean? What's wrong in playing with dolls?" I got up, dusted my jeans, and walked to him.

"What's wrong with playing football?" Avinash walked further towards me, his hands in his pocket.

"Nothing. Absolutely nothing. It's wonderful. No, not playing with football or playing with dolls...it's wonderful to do what you love, to be yourself."

"What do you know about football?" he grimaced, staring at my leg.

"Avinash!" Avni's voice was sharp as she walked towards us. "I love this doll, Vivaan, and I always loved dolls more than I ever loved football," she said with a determination I didn't know resided in her. She was being herself at that moment.

Avinash was clearly unhappy and after a loaded silence, he said, "Avni, I am going home. Are you coming?" She wasn't being herself anymore when she nodded. Avinash walked out and Avni followed him. I shook my head, but she mouthed 'sorry' and walked away.

Pain had settled in her eyes and I just wanted to erase it bit by bit, but in the little time I got with her in college, that too with Avinash looming around the corner, it wasn't possible. So one day I asked her out for coffee. "Is it a date?" She had asked me. "You can think so," I had replied.

So, I reached the restaurant right on time, but she was already there waiting for me.

"Hey, I thought girls were supposed to be late." I teased her, taking my seat across her.

"I didn't know that. This is my first date. But be ready to wait next time." She shifted on her seat, clearly nervous for this first date. She looked ravishing in her sleeveless white top and fitted black skirt.

"You look gorgeous."

"Thanks," she whispered, nervously adjusting her hair. After a long time, traces of pain left her eyes, and the forgotten smile was making its way back to her lips.

We had hardly talked for a few minutes when an unexpected voice startled us. "Hey, what a coincidence!" On second thought, it shouldn't have been unexpected. I let out a sigh before turning towards him.

"Hey, Avinash. Coincidence? Yeah, sure." I tried to hide my disappointment with a forced smile.

He joined us uninvited with all his friends and our first date turned into a group gathering of his friends.

Days merged into weeks and weeks to months, and this became a pattern. Avinash followed us like a shadow whenever I and Avni were together.

CHAPTER TWENTY-EIGHT

AVINASH

4 months Later

The park was eerily quiet at this time of the night. Sitting at the bench and watching the empty playground reminded me of my childhood. Avni loved swings. I did too, but since there were only two swings in the park and the other one was mostly occupied, I pretended to hate swings. Instead, I pushed her swing high in the air and she used to giggle and plead with me to go slow. I got into endless fights with other kids whenever they refused to give the swing to Avni, or when they made fun of her blunders. She was grown up now, but I still felt like she was the same little girl, fragile and sensitive. I was always scared someone would hurt her. But was I pushing her away with my protectiveness?

The argument reverberated in my mind. I had accused her of spending all her time with Vivaan and she said it wasn't her fault that I couldn't get a girlfriend. Seriously? I just walked out slamming the door. I didn't even reply to mom when she asked me where I was going.

"Hey bro." a voice came from behind me, but I refused to look at her. Avni came and sat next to me. Of course, she knew where to find me.

"I said some horrible things today," she said.

"Yes, you did," I didn't look at her.

"I am sorry, I didn't mean it."

"Do you know Priyanka proposed to me last week?" Avni needed to know it's not that I won't get a girlfriend, it's just that I wasn't yet ready for a relationship. And when it comes to commitment, I wanted to be sure. I wouldn't experiment with someone's sentiments.

"What?" she exclaimed, and when I finally faced her, she was looking at me wide-eyed. "How can you even complain that I hide things from you?"

"You got to know it from me, not from someone else. Moreover, you don't have time for me now."

"Whatever! So, what did you reply?" She turned towards me, folded her legs on the bench, and stared at me curiously. I was not completely wrong that she was still a little girl.

"Of course, I am not interested."

"Why?"

"She's not my type. You know, she once told me that I should stop being the over-possessive brother and focus on my own life."

I didn't tell Avni that I had a crush on Priyanka, but I once overheard Priyanka referring to Avni as 'that messy girl,' and that was the point my crush ended. A girl who didn't like my sister could never be my girlfriend.

"What? Why are you smiling?" I asked her.

"Over possessive!" she laughed.

"Yeah, yeah." I dramatically nodded. "I know the whole world thinks that I am an over-possessive brother but I don't give a damn about what people think."

"Cool down, Avinash. But let me tell you one thing. Even I don't like her. And by the way, what's your type of girl?"

And just like that, all our differences evaporated as we sat on that bench discussing topics that were new to us.

"Why do you always walk out of home after a fight?" she asked me on our way home.

"To calm down my mind."

"Why do you get so angry so fast?"

"But didn't you notice I cool down just as fast?"

She just smiled at that. Just a word from her calms my mind down.

Mom scolded us when we reached home. She had called us endlessly, but Avni forgot her phone at home and mine was silent. "Now go to sleep. Tomorrow is Raksha Bandhan, you need to get up early." Mom said and went to her room.

Early in the morning, after saying our prayers, Avni applied *tika* on my forehead and tied a thread rakhi on my hand—the kind I preferred, because it was easier to keep.

"Now remove the older one," she said and was about to tug the older one off, but I pulled my hand back. "It will wear out on its own." I didn't look at her but I knew she was smiling.

I walked to the closet and hesitantly pulled out the gift. Did I select too girly things?

"This is for you." I turned to her. She looked at me dumbfounded for a second before she grabbed the gift.

"Pink?" she exclaimed.

"I thought you like pink," I said and walked to the small bed at the end of the room.

"Of course, I like pink." She sat down next to me and excitedly opened the wrapping, and out spilled the ridiculously pink things—a frilly top, a hairband, a pink bracelet, and pink earrings. What was I thinking when I brought her these silly things?

"Coming in a minute," she said and disappeared inside her room. When she returned, I couldn't stop laughing.

"Oh my God, Avni. Don't you think it would have looked better on a five-year-old?" Mom was also laughing hysterically.

"Staying so many years with a blunder queen has to make a blunder king," I teased her. "If you want, I can get these exchanged."

"No!" she shrieked, hugging herself in her pink top. "I love it." Why did I even think she would exchange any gift from me, though she must know how stupid she looked.

"Then you must wear it outside also, not only at home. Okay?" I teased her.

She hesitated but quickly replied, "Definitely. But you are not going to get away with that. Give me your hand." She walked up to me with some horrendous plan.

"You have already tied the rakhi." I pulled both my hands behind my back.

"Give me your hand." She commanded and pulled out a ridiculously big Spiderman Rakhi from her pocket.

"No way." I jerked back.

"If you want, you can remove it later." She smiled mischievously, pulling my hand forcefully. She knew I would never remove her rakhi.

"Don't you think it's too small?" I said in mock anger, letting her tie it to my hand.

"Yeah, but I couldn't find anything smaller than this." She tied the rakhi, pulled out her mobile and clicked my photo with that stupid rakhi, posted it on Facebook, and tagged all my friends. I also clicked her photo with all the ridiculously pink things, posted it on Facebook, and tagged all her friends.

Then we smiled for a selfie as I highlighted the Spiderman Rakhi and she flaunted her absurdly pink things.

It was the stupidest of all our photos,

And the loveliest too.

I looked at Avni while she arranged her hairbands and other things in her dressing table. She was still my little sister, but as much as I hated it, she was grown up. She took some important decisions in her life and I was proud to admit she took the right decisions. I had been rude to Vivaan, but I needed to check his patience. After witnessing so much pain in my mom's life, the last thing I could tolerate for Avni was a short-tempered man. But Vivaan's patience was unbelievable. I planned to talk to him on the camping tour. I was convinced he was the right choice, but I still needed one heart-to-heart conversation with him before making up my mind. I wanted surety that my sister would be happy with him. And until then, I wasn't going to leave them alone for too long. I couldn't help that I loved my sister and I couldn't, just couldn't, stop worrying about her. After settling this, I would be ready for a relationship.

I never wrote Avni a letter after I turned eight, but for some reason, I wanted to gift her a letter again, but I decided to gift her that letter after talking to Vivaan and being sure of my decision.

I walked to my room and after almost a decade I wrote a letter.

"Hey Blunder Queen..." I started writing.

CHAPTER TWENTY-NINE

VIVAAN

Mom was humming a sad song, but she didn't realize it. The distant look in her eyes while she was tying rakhi to Lord Krishna meant she was with her late brother. Then suddenly she stopped humming, her hands froze on the rakhi, and I was sure she was lost somewhere in the time that was long gone. She once told me the memories of her time with her brother had blurred and she hated herself for that She wasn't trying to fight back her tears because there were none. Sometimes people cry without tears.

"What happened, Mumma?" Kanha asked, sitting cross-legged in front of the prayer shrine, waiting for his turn.

"Why aren't you a girl?" She was quick to shift her focus; she was mastering this art year after year. "If I had a daughter, she would be tying your rakhi and not me." Kanha looked bewildered, sucking his lollipop.

"It's not yet late if you want a daughter." Dad winked at mom and she punched him on his stomach playfully.

After mom tied us rakhi, we sat down for breakfast. My phone flashed with a message from Avni. She shared a photo where two grown-up twins still believed they were just five and I couldn't stop smiling.

"I am sure it's a message from Avni." Mom teased me. "Because you are smiling. I want to meet this girl who taught my grumpy son to smile," she said, passing the sandwich to me. She was so happy when I told her I was seeing Avni.

"Mom, I was never grumpy. Okay?"

"But you were the serious kind, for sure."

I didn't argue because she was right. It was not just mom, a lot of people told me that I had changed for the better, that I was smiling more.

I showed her the photo and mom laughed. "Aw! She's so adorable. Bring her home soon; I am tired of living with three odd boys," she said, looking at me, Kanha, and dad one by one. Dad peeped over her shoulder to look at the photo. "Kanha won't have to search for friends outside," Dad said light-heartedly referring to her childish behavior.

After breakfast, I met Arjun at the hospital as he was supposed to receive the latest reports of his dad. He was standing outside the doctor's cabin, staring at the report with wet eyes. I walked towards him cautiously, dreading to ask about the report. He looked up at me, nodded, and hugged me fiercely. "Dad is fine. His reports are good. He beat cancer!" His voice faltered. I patted his back and nodded. I was so happy I couldn't utter a word. But we never shared our feelings through words, we never had to. We still had to pay the huge debt we took as loan, but his reports were a huge relief.

"I can't wait to show these reports to dad," he said, and I could already witness a change in his persona. The lines of constant worry etched on his face faded and his eyes held hope, just like the old days. We walked outside the hospital and discussed our plans to repay the loan.

Finally, life was falling in place and it would have continued that way had I failed to convince Avni to join me for the two-day camping trip arranged by a few students on the campus. No teachers were involved, so the parents were apprehensive. I coaxed Avni to join and she, in turn, convinced Avinash. Her mother didn't want to risk not informing his dad who was on a business tour, but finally, she agreed. Little did we know that those two days would stretch to infinity, changing our lives forever.

CHAPTER THIRTY

AVNI

It was surreal.

I was on my way to spend two days with Vivaan. He was sitting at the window seat and I was sitting beside him. Avinash was sitting in the next seat after the aisle. After a sincere apology from Shreyansh, things were fine between us. Avinash never wanted to befriend him again but when I insisted, they became friends again. And I was glad for it since Shreyansh never misbehaved after that. When our bus passed through a slum area, Vivaan got unusually quiet. I could see his lips twitching when a beggar child ran behind a car.

"Do you love kids?" he looked at me unexpectantly. I adjusted to the sunlight coming from the window to look at his sad face.

"Kids? Yes. Why?"

"Thank God." He sighed and stared back out of the window. I could see his gaze rested on another abandoned kid sitting with a bowl at a crossroad. "Our child will never feel unwanted, unloved."

Irrespective of how it sounded, his words weren't romantic; they were sad. I held his arm with my both hands and rested my head on his shoulder. "You will make a great dad, Vivaan." It was kind of odd saying that to him, but I had to. He patted my hand and rested his head on mine.

"So, how many kids do you want?" he asked.

This time his words weren't sad and they sent tingles down my spine. This time it wasn't about his past, it was about us. When I didn't reply, he stared at me, demanding a reply.

"Two," I said, wishing he would stop staring at me like that. When he didn't stop staring, I asked him, "What?"

"I want a dozen."

I gasped and I hated that his expression didn't change a bit. Anyone watching him from a distance could say he might be discussing politics, but the same person watching me might get right on it.

"Shut up!" I fisted him playfully on his arm and rested my head back on his shoulder, so he would stop staring at me like that. My heart was still running at the speed of an Express train, but it came to a sudden halt when I saw Avinash's reflection in the front mirror, staring hard at us. I jerked back, putting some distance between me and Vivaan.

Soon, Avinash walked up to us. "I am nauseous. I might need to throw up. Can I exchange my seat with you Vivaan?" I knew Avinash was lying and I was sure Vivaan also knew that, but he just nodded and got up from the seat. I knew Vivaan was upset, and his irritation was justified. Avinash never allowed us privacy of more than fifteen to twenty minutes. Today, I was looking forward to spending at least a few hours of the six-hour-long journey together, but just after twenty minutes, Avinash pulled us apart. Vivaan never complained about how Avinash often commented on his leg. The only argument I ever had with Vivaan was regarding Avinash's control over me. Vivaan wanted me to take a stand, but sometimes he failed to understand that Avinash was not possessive, he was just protective.

Vivaan rested his head on the back of his new seat and closed his eyes. I sent him a text message: "You look hot when you are angry!"

He didn't pull out his phone from his pocket to check the message, so I called him. When he pulled out his phone from his pocket, I disconnected so he knew I wanted to say something. He checked his messages but didn't smile as I expected. He put his phone back in his pocket, folded his hands over his chest, and closed his eyes.

"Avni, do you remember we visited this temple once when we were kids?" Avinash pointed outside the window pulling my attention to him.

"Didn't you want to throw up?" My tone was harsher than I intended. He glared at me and then didn't talk to me the whole way. The long journey passed with the two important people of my life mad at me for no mistake of mine. And I didn't make any further effort to appease any of them.

We reached the camping site at eight and set our tents. Avinash and Shreyansh were sharing a tent. I was sharing a tent with Priyanka. Vivaan was going to share his tent with Arjun, but Arjun had to cancel his plan at the last hour so Vivaan had the tent to himself. Later in the night, we all gathered out around a campfire. The air was cold and crisp, and the camping site was surrounded by lots of trees. The tour guide warned us not to go outside the camping site, due to the danger from wild animals.

Vivaan was looking into his mobile when I reached him. "Hey, angry young man." I teased him but he didn't look at me.

I nudged him on his stomach. "Are you ticklish?" But he still didn't look up from his phone.

"Now stop being grumpy for no reason."

"No reason?" He finally looked at me. "Why are you here talking to me? Your toddler brother will pounce on us any minute. It's been months, Avni. Sometimes I am allowed to feel bad. Right?'

"I know, but..."

"But what, Avni?"

"I will talk to him."

"When?" he questioned.

"Now you are being unreasonable. I will talk to him after returning home. I don't want to spoil this evening, Vivaan. Please understand."

Vivaan never lost his temper, but for the last few days Avinash's behavior was constantly putting him off and I couldn't blame him. He was about to say something in that scary expression of his, but as soon as he saw the tears brimming in my eyes, he pulled me in a friendly hug, "I am sorry, I overreacted." This was the best thing about Vivaan—he never got mad, and whenever he did, it wasn't for long.

He kissed me on my hair and whispered, "Let's get out of here." The camping site was secured with railings and when we tried to walk out of the site, the guide stopped us at the exit.

"It's risky out there."

"We will be nearby," Vivaan said.

"The jungle is dense. You can lose your way even a few feet from here, and you know what's worse, there's hardly any network here."

Vivaan nodded in understanding and we walked back to the campfire. By now, almost everyone had resigned to their tents. Only ten to fifteen people were left, including Avinash.

We sat down near the campfire; the warmth of the rising flames against the cold air was refreshing. The sounds of the chirping insects and the trees dancing to the wind were beautiful. I turned towards Vivaan to say something but my voice hitched in my throat at the way Vivaan was staring at me.

"You know, I have often imagined you in a red gown." He caressed my cheek with a feathery touch, looking down at my red gown, and then up at my face, a deep primal hunger evident in his eyes.

"Really?" I didn't know what I wanted -for him to look away or to keep staring at me the whole night.

"Why does that surprise you?" his fingers reached my lips, sending a wild tremor through me, "should I have imagined you without it?"

His lips didn't turn into a smile, he didn't hint he was joking. His stare didn't accelerate my breathing this time, it just stopped it. We were devouring each other with our eyes, when a sound from the background broke the spell.

"I am not the only one watching you." It was Avinash.

We pulled back with a jolt and I looked around. There weren't many people around us but those who were there were enjoying the free entertainment.

"You should go to you tent Avni," Avinash demanded and I was so embarrassed I just nodded. Without waiting Vivaan got up and walked towards his tent, obviously pissed off by Avinash's behaviour. I wished good night to Avinash and walked towards my tent, but stopped to say good night to Vivaan on my way.

He was lying on his bedding. His hands were clasped behind his head and his eyes were closed when I reached his tent. He had changed into his shorts and vests.

"Good night, Vivaan?" I bent in from the entrance and peeped inside.

"Good night." He said sternly, his eyes still closed.

"Avni, what are you doing here? It's late. Go to your tent."

Shit. Avinash. Let me breathe.

"I will leave in two minutes, Avinash!" I tried to keep calm though I was losing it.

"Avni, go to your tent." He commanded.

"Avinash, she is a grown-up girl. You don't always need to tell her what she must do." Vivaan's pitch wasn't loud but it was stern.

Avinash raised his eyebrow, walking inside the tent. No, no, no... this wasn't good. He froze when his eyes landed on Vivaan's leg. He wasn't wearing his prosthetic leg.

"You won't understand. You don't have a sister." Avinash said, still staring at his leg, his tone much more sarcastic than it ever had been.

Avinash, please grow up! Stop staring at him like that. I wanted to shout but I didn't voice my thoughts.

"You don't have a girlfriend, so you won't understand too." Vivaan stood up on his one leg, pulled up his support stick, and stared at Avinash. "Do you know how much you suffocate her?"

Oh God, this was not good. I had promised Vivaan that I would talk to Avinash. Why couldn't he wait for one more day?

"You told him that I suffocate you?" Avinash's eyes turned wide and his tone was emotionless, masking the hurt behind it. Before I could reply, Vivaan said, "She doesn't need to say it. It's obvious."

"Do I suffocate you, Avni?" Avinash ignored Vivaan's statement.

"Avinash...I," I fumbled for words, "I just wish...for some space."

The silence was heavy and brooding before Avinash broke it.

"I will give you the space you need, Avni. I will leave you forever."

Avinash said all kinds of stupid things when he was angry, but my stomach still flipped at his last words. Avinash turned around to leave when Vivaan's hand rested on his shoulder. "Grow up, Avinash. We didn't mean that."

Avinash pushed him hard and, unprepared for that sudden push, Vivaan stumbled on the tools he had used to set up the tent.

"Avinash, wait!" I walked behind him but before I could step out, Vivaan's words stabbed me.

"Sometimes, I feel our relationship can never prosper as long as Avinash is there."

No matter how angry I was with Avinash, Vivaan's statement put me off. I spin around to yell at him, but he was lying on the floor, blood dripping from the end of his leg where he used to attach his prosthetic leg. The pointed broken edge from a tool had pierced his leg when Avinash pushed him.

"Oh my God, Vivaan. You're bleeding." I ran up to him.

"You don't need to care for me. Go, your brother needs you."

"Can we fix up your wound first and save the taunts for later?"

I went to my tent and got the first aid kit. Vivaan was lying on the small bedding with his eyes closed and his hands clasped behind his head when I returned. The wind was fierce that so I pulled up the zipper of the tent. I cleaned his wound and applied Dettol before tying a bandage around it. I was looking at the bandage when Vivaan said, "It's not a good sight, I know." His eyes were still closed.

"Not a part of your body is bad to look at. Okay?"

"How do you know about the other parts?" His tone was neutral, but somehow, his lips stretched to a grin, and just like that, the tension between us evaporated.

"You pervert!" I bent down to hit him on the chest, but he held my hand and pulled me in. Unprepared, I fell over him and my body went up in flames at the unexpected intimacy. I slowly slid and lay down next to him, and we turned to face each other. He closed his eyes and pulled my hand to his chest; his heart was beating erratically. Slowly, hesitantly, I pulled his free hand so he could feel my own erratic heartbeat and with that touch our heartbeats accelerated.

The warm glow of the dim light on his face added to the lure of the moment. He pushed his hand in my hair and pulled me in for a hungry kiss. We had kissed before, but we had never been so close, lying side by side on the same bed. And as we tasted each other like never before, our connection escalated to a new level. I was scared my heart would rip open with the overflowing love and I pulled back, but his arm snaked around my waist and pulled me towards him. His eyes bored into me, "I told you I always imagined you in a red gown." I swallowed, remembering what he had said next. He traced my face with his fingers and with his feathery touch, my desire shot to a whole new level. His hands didn't stop at my chin, it travelled down my neck and yet below, until it reached my neckline. But then it stopped. I should have stepped back, should've left his tent, but instead, I pulled his hand to where his eyes were fixed, sliding it beneath my gown. His warm touch filled me with pleasure so intense that a small moan escaped my throat. And then there was no stopping. Within no time our hands were exploring more of each other, removing the hurdles between us. The distance between us melted inch by inch, piece by piece, until we unraveled every little secret of each other, until we finally molded into one, like long lost pieces of the same puzzle.

CHAPTER THIRTY-ONE

VIVAAN

My heart thumped with passion, love, longing, hunger and a thousand different emotions as my body melted into her as if she was my home. Home was just a word for me until now, but now it had a meaning, a name. Avni.

It was a trance, and once out of that trance, Avni was trembling the whole time she put on her clothes, combed her hair with her fingers, slipped on her sandals and walked towards the exit. And during the whole time, she avoided looking at me.

"Avni!" I called out when she was about to leave. "You are not guilty, right?"

Her hand froze at the zipper of the tent but she didn't turn around to look at me.

"Avni, look at me, please."

She hesitantly faced me, but her eyes still didn't meet mine.

I got up, picked up my support stick, and walked to her. "Look at me." It broke me that she flinched just at the brush of my finger. "I love you!" I hugged her and she started crying, shrinking in my hug. "I am not letting you leave unless you stop crying, I don't want you to regret the most truthful moments between us." I stroked her back until she stopped trembling. Once she calmed down, she pulled apart, her eyes fixed on the door.

"It's late. I should leave now."

I didn't want her to leave, but since it was too late, I just nodded and followed her.

"Where are you going?" she asked me.

"You can't expect me to let you go alone at this time. I will walk you to your tent."

"It's just a few feet, Vivaan. And it's not a good idea to let anyone see us together at this time."

I nodded thoughtfully, but still followed her out of my tent. Suddenly, I was terrified with the prospect of our silhouettes being visible from outside, but fortunately, the tent being thick, nothing was visible. Also, most of the surrounding tents were dark.

When Avni turned in a different direction than her tent, I asked her, "Where are you going?"

I followed her gaze that pointed at Avinash's tent.

"For God's sake, Avni! For once in your life, can you stop thinking about your..." I tried to suppress my irritation. But maybe I was being unreasonable. If I stopped Avni from doing what she wanted, how was I any different than Avinash? But before I could apologize, she turned back and walked to her tent.

CHAPTER THIRTY-TWO

AVNI

I just wanted to say good night to Avinash. More than that I couldn't bear to look into his eyes. We fought endless times but never slept without making up. He must have expected me to see him before he went to sleep, and a simple good night would calm down his anger. But I didn't want to annoy Vivaan so I walked to my tent.

When I entered my tent, Priyanka was reading something on her mobile.

"Enjoying the trip, it seems," she winked at me.

"Yeah, enjoying," I said stubbornly and lay down next to her on the mattress, turning my back to her so she couldn't see me. I pretended to sleep, but sleep eluded me. The moments with Vivaan had changed something inside me, like his love was now sealed in my soul, had become permanent. The memory was beautiful and yet draped with guilt.

After hardly sleeping for three to four hours, I got up at six. The weather was dreamy with the chatter of birds lingering in the fresh air, but despite feeling relaxed, an uncanny feeling crawled over me. I got up with a jolt and walked to Avinash's tent.

"Avinash!" I called out. There was no response.

"Avinash!" I called out louder. But there was still no response. I dialed his number but it was unreachable. I called out louder this time and Shreyansh walked out, rubbing his eyes. When I asked about Avinash, he suddenly jolted out of his sleep.

"Oh shit!" Shreyansh ran his hand through his hair, "Avinash walked out at 1 a.m. I warned him that it was risky outside, but he said he needed some fresh air and would return in a while. I was too tired so I slept immediately."

"Shit. Are you crazy?" I screamed at him.

"Don't worry, he must be around," Shreyansh said, but the tremble in his voice unleashed the panic rising inside me. I stormed to Vivaan's tent. He came out when I called out his name.

"Vivaan, Avinash is not in his tent."

He rubbed his eyes. "Stop worrying like he's a real toddler." He pulled me towards him, but I pushed him apart.

"It's six in the morning and he left his tent at almost one. He was not here at night." I pointed my finger vaguely outside the camping area. "He was out somewhere in the wild. Do you understand?" I shouted.

"What?" Vivaan was suddenly alert. Without wasting a second, he grabbed his prosthetic leg and fixed it. We rushed from tent to tent, shouting Avinash's name, but he was nowhere.

"He was upset when he left the tent at one," Shreyansh said.

By this time, I had lost my calm and I was trembling all over.

"Cool down, Avni. I am sure Avinash is alright." Vivaan touched my shoulder, but I pulled back with a jerk. If only he didn't stop me from talking to him last night; Avinash had left Shreyansh's tent just fifteen minutes later. He must be upset after the fight and must have walked out to calm down his mind. He often did that whenever he was upset.

"Avinash!" My throat had started aching as I kept shouting and running like a maniac in the forest. Soon it was only me and Vivaan.

"Avni, control yourself. We are in a forest. If we forget the directions, we can get lost. Our group is left far behind."

"That's all you can think of?" I pointed a finger at him, "when my brother is God knows where? That we can lose directions? I don't care a damn! Do you understand that? I love my toddler brother more than you can think. Do you understand that?" I screamed.

"I understand that Avni, but getting lost in the forest is not going to help us reach Avinash. We have to be practical and search for him."

I was in no mood to argue, so I continued with my search, shouting Avinash's name through the dense forest. Soon, we reached a small lake, with a warning sign dangling to a tree, "Beware of alligators". I was walking inside the danger zone when Vivaan pulled me back. "Are you crazy? This is a danger zone."

"I don't care. Leave me alone." I cried, and suddenly a panic rose inside me. What if Avinash came here at night and didn't see the warning sign? Amid a thousand ugly thoughts, my mind held hope, brushing aside my stupid pessimistic theories.

But only until I saw it. The ridiculously big Spiderman Rakhi.

And his phone, a piece of a blue shirt—his shirt—drenched in blood. And a trail of blood...leading to Avinash lying face down.

In a pool of blood.

No...no...no...it couldn't be happening! My legs betrayed me when I wanted to run down to him, my bloody voice also betrayed me when I wanted to shout his name. As if in a daze, I heard Vivaan shouting, "Oh shit...oh shit!"

Vivaan was near Avinash the next moment, turning him on his back. Avinash didn't react; his body simply adjusted to Vivaan's movements. Vivaan patted his cheek but Avinash didn't respond. Vivaan tried to feel his pulse...then Vivaan kept his fingers beneath Avinash's nose but his face turned pale and he shook his head.

A loud cry escaped my throat that somehow failed to reach my ears. It was eerily silent, only my heartbeats in the dead silence. I felt as if I was in a vacuum, as if it wasn't real, as it was a dream and I would wake up any moment.

The world was a blur, receding to darkness...and I couldn't define the moment when I disconnected from this useless world.

I will leave you forever...

Someone was calling out a name...my name...

Avni...the voice had a faraway feel as if coming from a different world.

Where was I? Why was everything a blur?

When the blur cleared, I was on Vivaan's lap and he had tears in his eyes....tears?

Avinash...

It took me a while to find my voice. "Tell me it's a lie. That it isn't what I thought it to be. Tell me Avinash is fine...just injured." I grabbed Vivaan's collar "Tell me he is fine. Tell me!" As my voice echoed in the wilderness, a strange numbness took over me.

I pushed Vivaan away when he was about to hug me. "Where is he?" I asked.

He pointed his finger in Avinash's direction. Some people surrounded him. Were those our friends or strangers? Why does it even matter?

We were outside the danger zone.

When did we reach here? How long had I been unconscious?

Avinash looked fine—his face was serene, the cold breeze was ruffling his wild brown hair, his dark eyes were closed but his skin was fresh as the morning. He looked as if he was just sleeping peacefully. Vivaan was probably mistaken; Avinash was fine.

But I dreaded touching Avinash as if a single touch would change everything. When I touched him, his skin was cold. I pulled up his head but it fell when my grip loosened.

I fisted his shirt and put my head on his chest, scared, still waiting for a miracle, still waiting to hear the tiniest beat of his heart. God, please God, please!

There wasn't a beat...not even the slightest.

I will leave you forever.

My mind was shutting down. The sounds came to me in waves.

"Lot of bleeding...crocodile attack...escaped from the attack...too much blood loss..."

"Went out for a short walk, but might have forgotten the directions..."

"Ambulance is coming..."

A hand touched my shoulder, maybe held it. And the next moment I was in the ambulance. What happened? Where was Avinash? He was sleeping on the stretcher.

Sleeping...wasn't it easier to say it that way?

Except, there was no easy way anymore.

Thankfully, the blood was cleaned. He had a blood phobia.

Had.

How long had it been?

Much of the journey passed in a daze, some voices rumbled around, someone patted my back constantly. It was Priyanka, I guess, but what did it matter? All that mattered was that it wasn't Avinash consoling me after a disaster like every other time. His hand around my shoulder was missing, the slight tap on my head teasing me, calling me blunder queen was missing. His absence in my life was forever. I held Avinash's cold hand all the way long. How long before this small comfort would be taken away too? People around me kept saying stupid things about courage and all...things that were baseless, hollow, empty.

It took us a decade to reach home. I wanted to rush into mom's arms but how would I face her? I was the one who convinced her to let us go. If I hadn't convinced her, if I hadn't gone into Vivaan's tent at that late hour, if I had gone to wish Avinash good night, if I had called him after returning to my tent...If I had done even a single thing out of the innumerable possibilities, I wouldn't be dragging my feet to my home alone.

There were a lot of people at home when I reached. Mom and dad were waiting at the gate.

"First, I came first!" A memory creeped up to me out of nowhere. At this very gate, Avinash had said those words a million times during our silly, childish quest of being the first to reach the gate.

Now those words would never be spoken again. Never.

"Avinash!" Mom's voice echoed endlessly in the eerie silence as she frantically hugged Avinash, kissing him all over his face. My head was throbbing. Dad was crying too, hugging him from the other side. I wasn't sure how long their voices echoed—a minute, an hour, or an eternity. All I remembered was that when I hugged mom, she didn't respond. And that crumbled the last straw of strength left in me.

Time was no more a fixed entity, it was volatile. The world was a blur, the air was scarce, the voices were muffled. The only concrete thing was the pain bursting forth from every molecule of my body, ripping me apart.

In that blur, some people were taking my brother away for his last rituals. "Wait!" I ran behind them. A few voices mumbled something.

Avinash looked handsome in his white kurta-pajama. When did they change his dress? I had teased him endlessly that any girl would fall for him whenever he wore a white kurta.

I held his hand for one last time...and tied the Spiderman Rakhi back on his wrist.

CHAPTER THIRTY-THREE

NIDHI

It was two in the morning when I heard some noise in Vivaan's room. He still couldn't sleep. I walked up to his room and as expected, he was pacing around. His back was towards the door and in the dim light, his hunched-up frame broke my heart.

"Vivaan!" I called out.

"Mom?" he spun around.

"Again, the same nightmare?" I touched his shoulder.

"No, it's...it's different now." he stammered.

I knew just by the way he spoke that he was dreaming of Avinash and Avni and the horrible incident. I sat down on the bed and he sat on the floor, resting his head on my lap, just like he did when he was a kid.

"It's been two weeks, Mom. I want to be there for Avni, but she doesn't even want to see me."

"Avni said that?" I stroked his hair.

"She doesn't need to. It's written all over her face. She jerks back whenever I try to console her. She didn't even look at me and once when she did, I...her...eyes...shouted that I killed her brother!"

"Don't say that, Vivaan!"

Vivaan hadn't stammered in a long time. In more than a decade, in fact.

"What hurts me more than the look in her eyes is that...that..." His voice cracked. "It's true."

His words reflected the feelings I had nurtured for a long time until Noel came into my life. "Don't say that, Vivaan. Don't let that thought make a place in your heart ever."

"It's already a part of my system. How can it not be? Avni wanted to talk to him when he walked out of our tent, but I stopped her and..." He didn't say anything for a long time and I knew he had a lump in his throat.

"It was destiny," I said, feeling the hollowness of my own words.

"Why is destiny always unfair to me?" Vivaan's voice cracked as he looked up. Even in the dim light, his eyes reflected loss. He looked like the seven-year-old Appu—broken and hopeless. And a strange fear grabbed me. He was receding to the same darkness we had pulled him out of. He was talking his heart out, something he never did anymore. It should have made me happy but to say the truth, it scared me. Because if he was sharing, it meant he was losing control.

"Yesterday, when I visited her with our other friends, she appeared smaller, as though she had shrunk in size. She was huddled in a corner, oblivious to her surroundings." Vivaan hid his face in my lap.

That defines you too, I wanted to say, but I didn't voice my thoughts. With his weight loss, the dark circles around his eyes, and a constant worry line on his forehead, the loss was now etched on his persona.

"She didn't respond when Priyanka tried to talk to her, but she... she... jerked away violently when I placed my hand on her shoulder."

"Give her some time, she will understand you someday."

"Her phone is switched off. She isn't even coming to college. How am I...I...ever going to tell her how sorry I am, how awful I feel?"

"She will talk to you. Don't worry." I gave him the hope I didn't hold. This was a life-changing incident, the kind that changed the core of a person. She might no longer be the Avni he had loved. Even if she came back, there would always be an accusation in her eyes. And it was difficult to say what was worse—losing a person completely or living with the shell of a person you loved but then lost.

"Will Avni also leave me like my..." He forced himself to stop. My hands stopped stroking his hair. Despite everything, I could never be his mother. But I didn't blame him. We came to his rescue after almost everything was ruined. We left him with strangers, something a mother would never do.

In his painting, the one where a little bird was waiting for his mother in the lonely nest, I often thought it was him waiting for his mother. But isn't it true that he had often caught me staring at the broken egg shells hidden beneath the dried leaves? Did he know what my miscarriages did to me before Kanha came? Did he know that maybe, I was also waiting?

When he tried meeting his mother, he wasn't wrong. That much I knew from experience, even though it did hurt.

Our relationship might not have been perfect, but our love was. I knew he loved me, though not the way I wanted him to. I generally didn't look for cracks and focused on what I got. But sometimes, in tiny moments like these, I lost it.

"I am sorry, Mom" Vivaan's voice cut through my reverie and I resumed stroking his hair.

"It's ok, Vivaan." He didn't speak for a long time and the lump in my throat didn't allow me to speak as well.

I heard Kanha crying and I got up to leave.

I walked down to Kanha and lay down next to him. He snuggled to me, punching me with his small fist.

"Where did you go? Why did you leave me? I am not going to talk with you."

He started crying, staring at me with accusations, but a strange satisfaction filled me.

Kanha never searched for anyone else when he looked at my face.

CHAPTER THIRTY-FOUR

VIVAAN

While waiting for hours outside Avni's class, despite Arjun telling me she hadn't come, I realized time was vague. There were exactly sixty seconds in every minute and sixty minutes in every hour, but each second could carry the weight of eternity. Each second could last long enough to never end.

Finally, one day Avni returned to college, or maybe the person who returned was a mere shell of the Avni I knew. Her hair was tangled, just like her life. The darkness in her life had spilled over to form a layer beneath her eyes. Her white T-shirt and blue jeans, that used to fit her curves, were dangling around her frame. Hugging her bag to her bosom and her eyes focused on the ground, Avni walked as if the world around her scared her.

A world without Avinash.

Avni tripped over a stone but didn't bounce back like she did the first time we met. She stood there lost as if waiting for someone to tease her...

Blunder Queen.

She didn't cry. The girl who cried and laughed at the drop of a hat was gone. A strange void radiated from her and reached me in ripples. I just wanted to gather her in my arms, share the pain she wasn't capable of bearing alone, but I couldn't take a single step towards her. My legs had jammed, and I just watched her leave.

I silently followed her for a few days, fighting the constant lump in my throat, but after a few days I called out to her. Something flickered in her eyes, but she didn't look up. She just stormed away as if my voice stung her.

She left me calling out her name enough times. But it wasn't only me she avoided. She avoided people in general and instead of making me sad it gave me some comfort; she wasn't angry with me alone and someday, when she would accept the world, she would accept me back in her life.

With each passing day my patience withered. Seventy-five days had passed since Avinash was gone.

Since Avni was gone.

Arjun readily agreed to my plea and somehow brought Avni to the deserted porch—our secret meeting area, but as soon as Avni saw me, she froze, and Arjun left without turning back.

"Avni!" I reached her, but her eyes didn't budge from the spot on the ground. "Listen to me. For God's sake, please listen to me!" But before I could say sorry, she looked at me and my voice got stuck in my throat. There wasn't a single emotion in her eyes. *Not a single emotion*. Her eyes looked hollow.

"Who are you?" she asked.

Her words shook my world. It took me a moment to find my voice. "Avni, please don't say that. Please! I am sorry. Please listen to... to... me once." I touched her hand, but she violently jerked my hand as if my touch burned her. She turned around to leave, but how could I let her? My emotions switched from guilt, fear, and pain to anger. It had been months and I deserved one conversation with her. My relationship with her deserved this conversation. I forcefully pinned her to a tree and locked her within the bridges of my arms, staring right into her eyes.

"Just listen to me." My voice was harsh. "I am sorry, and I mean it." I swallowed the lump in my throat "I never knew it would turn so...so...bad, else I would have never stopped you."

"You remember what you said?" Her eyes challenged me. "You said, 'As long as Avinash is there our relationship can never prosper."

How could I forget that? Those words have reverberated endlessly in my lonely nights. "You know I didn't mean it."

"But it was our relationship because of which he..." Her voice faltered and she paused for a while. "And I mean it. How can you expect me to build my love life over Avinash's ashes? I hate you, Vivaan. I hate myself and I hate this stupid relationship of ours!"

Avni hates me! Her voice dangled in the space between us, that was now larger than infinity. Her words jolted through me, altering every molecule in my body. Until that moment, I didn't know words could be so damaging.

'I love you', she had told me once, her soft voice filling in the emptiness inside me. Now she had faded somewhere out of reach, into the dark recesses of the past.

Avni got out of my grasp and walked away. I couldn't follow her. Her words were too damaging for me. Too much. I stood there long after she left, just like the day I had stood there long after we had first accepted our love.

That night kept me awake, tossing and turning on my bed. But by the morning I was sure I could change Avni's mind. I would wait for her; it might be a day, a week, a year, or even a decade, but she would understand me someday and I would wait for her.

But reality soon jolted me out of my belief. One day, Arjun informed me that Avni had tried to end her life, that her condition was serious and she had been admitted to New Life Hospital. Arjun was still talking when I started running barefoot out of my gate, but then I turned back and took my bike. Within minutes I was at the hospital, but Avni's dad didn't let me reach her. Her dad reminded me of Avinash in some strange, uncomfortable way. Though Avni was discharged in a few days I couldn't see her. I spent hours in front of her class but she never returned. Her phone was constantly switched off.

The next news was that Avni had shifted to some other city to continue her studies. And then came the last jolt.

She was getting married.

That moment I knew one could die inside a living body.

Her ruthless words helped me to stay sane, hate her, and even tolerate her departure. But soon, very soon, her harsh words faded, her angry voice vanished, and her sweet voice and her innocent face were back to haunt me, to torment me with her absence. I tried some logical arguments, like after her indifferent behaviour I shouldn't have loved her, but alas! Love was not a business. There was no balance. There was always one who loved more. And in our relationship, it was me.

I spent hours and hours at the porch where our love had blossomed...and withered. I still watered the plant we had sown together. Her aura surrounded that place, her laughter still echoed in the air, her touch traveled through past and still comforted me in a strange way. And as I waited insanely for Avni, I felt like the seven-year-old Appu

who had waited at every crossroad for her mother.
But she never came.
Never.

CHAPTER THIRTY-FIVE

VEDIKA

"Munna!" My voice faltered as I lifted my son for the first time and my tears didn't stop.

"Munna, Munna!" I kept repeating his name, hugging him close, afraid that destiny would take him away. My husband's arm snaked around me, giving me the strength I needed, assuring me that Munna was here to stay. To my husband it was obvious, but for a woman who had to give away her first child, this was no less than a miracle.

The tears that were flowing were not only of happiness for holding my newborn baby, they also carried the pain of losing my first child. I didn't have the luxury to grieve then; I had to build a new life in a different city, far away from the place where my life had shifted gears. I wasn't sure what my life was going to be, and I didn't want that uncertainty to be a part of my son's life.

My newborn held my finger in his fist that was the size of a peanut, and a thousand emotions roared inside me, pushing me to a lost day twenty-two years back.

My pinkie was in his tiny fist. I had kissed his face endlessly before getting out of that grip. The pain was so intense that it could rip me apart. By some miracle, I gained the strength to walk away and hid behind a tree, waiting for someone to carry him to a different world—a world of orphans. But it was better than a life of a son whose father was a rapist and whose mother was the murderer of his father. There was no good life for him. I had to choose from the better among the worst.

I was about to run back to him when it started raining, but a lady opened the gate and picked him up, carrying him away to a world far away from my insecurities. And I regretted just one thing: that I could have kissed him one more time.

It took me more than eighteen years to trust another man, but love finally found me. I wanted to tell him everything, but I had already buried that part of my life so deep in my existence that I just couldn't let it resurface. It could destroy me. I married my love and my life was in place. Or so I thought. But what next? Motherhood?

I had a child I gave away. A child about whom I knew nothing.

I was already a mother.

Whenever my husband had shown his desire for parenthood, I pretended I loved freedom, but deep down I was a prisoner. A prisoner of the past.

And I never wanted to get free.

I always wanted to live in a bubble, that my firstborn was still the same innocent baby I gave away, unaware of the abandonment. But seeing him in front of me the other day had broken the façade. How did he manage to track me down? Was it from that one phone call I had made to the orphanage in a weak moment? The call I had dropped midway?

If he tracked it, he was looking for me.

He looked like his father. The moment I saw him in discotheque, I knew it was him. He had the same height, same complexion, same rugged features, same voice, and as much as I hate to admit it, the same charisma. But his eyes? His eyes weren't like him. They were kind and gentle. I didn't tell him that for obvious reasons.

No, I never wanted to know his name but after all, I was a mother. Maybe the worst one but still a mother. I checked his name from the hotel register.

Vivaan D'Souza.

The name and surname didn't match, but I liked the sound of his name. I remember uttering it many times.

Many.

I searched for him on social networking sites but he was nowhere.

Next, I searched his name on Google and finally, there he was. A painter. His paintings were splendid. I dug a little deeper and got the information about his family. They seemed like a happy family. I didn't want to cause trouble in his peaceful life, and yes, mine too. But seeing Munna liberated me in some strange way. It gave me closure. Well, he might have abandonment issues but at least he had a family to call his own, and I was content with that. And that was the day I decided I could become a mother once again.

As I went through his paintings, I realized he inherited his love for art from me. He also inherited the common pattern that followed my paintings after I gave him away.

All our paintings had something broken.

And hidden.

We were connected through those broken things.

But as love entered my life, those broken things disappeared slowly and I observed the same pattern in my son's paintings too.

But his last painting scared me—the one that was uploaded just two days back. It was loud and aggressive.

The kind I drew only once when I pushed his father from the thirtieth floor of the building. His father, my predator. Thankfully, the death was registered as an accident.

I was scared Munna would destroy himself or the source of his destruction.

God, please bless him. Keep him sane.

"Where are you?" My husband waved his hand in front of me.

"I was...am...with Munna," I said and kissed my newborn.

Part 2

10 Years Later

CHAPTER THIRTY-SIX

AVNI

"This is my favorite photo, madam," The maid said as she placed the photo frame back after dusting the table. In that nine-year-old photo, I and Dev were staring at each other, holding our hands.

I still remembered the day when he proposed to me. I didn't remember what he wore, or what expression reflected in his eyes, or where we were. I wasn't much observant in that phase of my life. What I remembered was the way he said 'I love you' had rippled across the waves of hollowness inside me.

'I love you too,' I had replied, too quick to be true. Maybe I was too eager to fill in the void inside me. Love was something I could never feel again. Or so I thought at the time. I lost the three most important people of my life together and each of them took away a part of me, and I needed someone to fill the gap. The void.

And more than anything, I needed to approve the boy chosen by my dad. This was the least I could do after all they went through because of me. Even after accepting his proposal, I was cut off most of the time but he was patient. I told him I had a past he might not like, but he said we all had a past and he didn't need to know about it. In return, he made me promise to never ask about his past. I was more than happy with the deal.

The early days of our marriage were tough. Sometimes when he spoke, his words didn't reach me. He needed to repeat almost everything to get my attention. Often, his face would blur behind some faraway memories and I would freeze amid a kiss. But the tenderness in his eyes never fazed. He would just hug me close and keep stroking my back, expecting nothing more than to calm down my racing heart. Anyone else in his place could have drifted away, but not Dev. His commitment was unfazed. And as time passed, I didn't realize when my heart began to sing the forgotten music once again, didn't realize when I started to smile and laugh and learned to be happy again. This photo was taken on the day we consummated our marriage. Yes, I was happy. I was ecstatic that day, that month, that year and for many years after that. Until...

"Mumma, I am back," Tia rushed into the room and hugged me after throwing her bag on the couch. It was her daily routine.

"How was your day honey?" I asked, pushing a strand of her hair behind her ears.

"Not very good. I fought with Manisha. She ate my chocolate and when I complained to ma'am, she was mad at me. She..."

I am not sure what she said after that. Absent-minded, I gave her verbal cues to let her know that I was listening, while my mind wandered through several things - about setting the table for lunch, checking Tia's homework, getting her to sleep by three so she could wake up by five.

"Mummy, you are not listening to me again!" Tia held my hand as I was undoing her shoelace.

"I am listening to you, Tia."

"Then tell me what I just said." She kept both hands on her waist, challenging me.

"That you fought with Manisha."

"Then?"

"You complained to your ma'am about it."

"Then?"

"Then...then..." I placed her shoes on the shoe rack and stood up. "Come on, it's time for lunch."

"Mumma, you never listen to me!"

"No, it's just that—"

"Leave it." She walked towards her toy room. "I will talk to Lilliput. She is my best friend. She always listens to me."

I told her to get fresh before picking up Lilliput, when I should have told her that I would listen to her, that she didn't need a lifeless doll to share her feelings with. But I didn't. How was I better than that emotionless doll! I was relieved that I could concentrate on other tasks without any disturbance.

"What's for lunch today?" Tia asked while playing with her doll.

"Pav bhaji," I said while setting her plate. Her toy room was direct across the dining room and I looked back when she started shouting.

"Yay! Yay!" Tia got up and started dancing. "You know what? Today Manisha brought garlic bread and she was teasing me that her papa takes her for a ride daily."

This was the innocence of a six-year-old. Forgetting and forgiving in minutes. I wish I could do that. Forgive her for the crimes she never committed.

After lunch, I made her bed and when she slept, I checked her homework. She got full marks in her class test. She was brilliant, just like her dad. After winding up my work, I woke her up at five and after drinking her milk, she was off to neighbor's place to play and I was relieved for I was with myself once again. I remembered the time when I liked to be with people. But of late, the people in my life failed to provide me any solace and I liked my own company. My phone rang when I was preparing dinner.

"Avni, I will be late today. Don't wait for me at dinner." Dev said, from the other end.

"Okay," I said tersely and disconnected the phone.

Our conversations were brief and to the point. No pleasantries, no joking around, just information sharing. It took me time to get used to it, but then it became comfortable. The familiarity of it was what made it comfortable. Whenever I desired a longer conversation, I was pulled back to the time when he tried to mend up the mess and more than that, the reason behind all the mess. And I just wanted things to go the way they were.

Tia returned in some time. After having dinner and making her do her homework, I made her bed.

"Mumma, it's storytime." Tia snuggled to me on the bed and put her arms on me. When I didn't respond, she pulled my hand to her waist so I was hugging her too.

"Which story do you want to listen to today?"

"Cinderella!" she chuckled.

"There was a girl called Cinderella. Her mother died when Cinderella was born and her step-mother didn't love her." My words always choked at this sentence. It took me a second to move on to the next line. As the story was about to end, I lingered a little longer on the word step-mother and I wasn't sure when I drifted to silence. But when I returned from my trance, Tia was asleep. My eyes lingered over her—her soft, tiny hands on my waist, her baby-soft skin, her pink lips, the warm glow on her face, the innocence. And all of it reflected just one thing; a glimpse of her mother's face. As usual, I slowly separated from her hug, turned my back to her, and tried to sleep.

CHAPTER THIRTY-SEVEN

AVNI

As Raksha Bandhan approached, a feeling of discontent engulfed me. But how long could I shut myself off in my room? Dev was on a business tour and I needed groceries, so I pushed myself to visit the market.

I dreaded the sight of the market decorated with colorful rakhis, from simple thread to big ones with twinkling lights. It opened the lid on memories I had boxed up in the deepest corners of my heart.

Defeating my will, my legs dragged me to a rakhi stall. I picked up a simple thread, the kind that Avinash preferred, the kind that could be worn long enough to another year. Once when his rakhi broke after tangling in a doorknob, Avinash had still preserved it.

"Mummy, I want that Spiderman Rakhi." A small voice reached my ears and my gaze traveled to the said rakhi on the corner of the stall. I reached out to it, touched it, lifted it. It trembled in my hand and all of it came alive. A lacy pink hairband, a big Spiderman Rakhi, two stupid siblings laughing nonstop into the camera. And then the same rakhi drenched in blood.

"Shall I pack this rakhi for you madam?" The words of the shopkeeper stabbed me. I shook my head and walked away before my tears became visible.

Without purchasing anything, I returned home and tried to focus on my daily chores, but I failed. I had tamed my mind to shut off the memories and it was long before I realized that when we shut off our mind to feel any pain, unknowingly, we also shut our mind to feel any joy.

In a trance-like state, I walked to my cabinet and opened it, pulled out the photo album from the bottom shelf, and wiped off the dust. And then I froze!

I didn't remember flipping the first page, I didn't remember when I started crying - at the first photo where two toddlers wearing the same attire were lying side by side holding hands, or when I saw two inseparable siblings cutting their fifth birthday cake. Despite holding the knife with one hand, he didn't miss out on putting two fingers behind my head. He never missed teasing me. Never.

A smile drenched in tears was the saddest smile I had ever known.

As I turned page after page, every photo reminded me how much we were a part of each other. Good memories on sad days are like stars studded in a dark night.

I reached the last page, the page I always dreaded—the photo of my last rakhi with him, the page where all the voices came alive.

"Don't you think it's too small?"

During our childhood, Avinash had gifted me a handmade card and a letter every year, but after eight he turned a little shy to express his feelings. But his love needed no words, no letters. The way he got protective of me said it all. My friends thought he was over-possessive, but I never saw it that way, at least not anymore when I long for someone to be protective of me.

A deep craving to see all that wasn't in the album surged somewhere in my heart. I and Avinash could no longer make new memories, so I had to preserve the ones I had. This battle with time was exhausting! It snatched away those precious moments piece by piece, blurring the views that were once prominent, and I wonder if I couldn't love him the way I should have.

I looked up at the sky. "Avinash..."

I spoke out his name aloud after a long time. It only made it worse, it made the loss evident. I talked aloud, as if he was sitting next to me. "No matter where you are or where I am, we were—and will always remain—connected. There is not a day in my life you are not with me. First, it was your presence around me and now, your memories that I turn to, to find solace. I wish you a happy life, I wish you a long life."

And I hugged the album tight and cried and cried and cried.

CHAPTER THIRTY-EIGHT

AVNI

I woke up with a jolt in the dark night, the words from my dream still fresh in my mind.

"You are pregnant."

The words dangled in the air, reminding me of the emptiness, of the yearning, of the hopelessness that hit me month after month when the test results came negative.

One mistake, or rather one sin. Maybe I deserved it.

Pulling me out of the darkness during the initial days of our marriage had taken a toll on Dev, I shouldn't have drifted back to the dark place again when I failed to conceive. But still, it didn't justify what Dev did.

I was pulled back to a day six years back, the day I never wanted to revisit, but the day that never stopped visiting me.

***

"It's time. Our baby may arrive any time. Please come soon." The accidental reading of that message had shaken my entire world. I had read the message repeatedly, trying to find some loopholes. But I failed to fool myself as Dev had replied, "will reach in half an hour." Dev had lied to me that he was

going out for some office work, and I hadn't doubted him, despite it being a Sunday evening.

He walked out of the washroom and announced, "I am leaving. I will be late." He had said, picking up his wallet from the drawer, and his phone from the bed, not looking at me all the while.

He didn't notice my silence or me not walking him to the gate to see him off, as I always did. Of course, his priority had shifted.

But when he reached the door, I forced myself up and followed him with a fragile hope that he would turn back once, but he didn't. He got into his car and drove away, and suddenly, like a maniac, I started running behind his car when he was far away.

"Want to go somewhere, madam?" A taxi driver stopped beside me.

I nodded and got into the taxi, pointed at the car, but couldn't say anything.

"Madam, are you ok?" the driver asked, and only then did I realize I was breathing hard, sweating all over, with an unusually tight grip on the seat belt. I hadn't even bothered to change out of my home clothes.

"Yes," I lied, loosening my grip over the seat belt.

After some time, Dev parked his car in front of a hospital and stormed inside. Only after I got out of the taxi did I realize I didn't carry my purse. Damn!

The kind man looked at my face for a second, at my folded fist around my sides for another, then back at my face.

"It's ok, madam. I was coming this way only."

Somehow, I mumbled thanks and rushed inside. I found Dev in the hallway talking to the doctor.

"Congratulations, you have a daughter." Those words of the doctor stabbed me, ripped me apart, and I stumbled back,

leaning on the wall. "But I am sorry. Mehak doesn't have much time."

Dev's back was towards me, but from the way his shoulders rounded, I knew he was broken. Though not as much as me. He was going to lose someone, and I had already lost someone. Thankfully, there were quite a few disheveled people in the lobby—someone running beside a stretcher, someone calling out another doctor, so it was easy to blend into the crowd. Dev entered a private room and with trembling legs, I followed him. I stood outside the room as the door was half-closed.

"I am sorry, Mehak. I am so so sorry. I have been so awful to you." The tremble in Dev's voice broke me. He feared losing her. He feared being lonely.

Lonely with me.

"It's not the time to apologize, Dev." Her soft voice hit me like a tornado, "what was a moment of weakness for you was a moment of love for me. I never wanted to burden you, but the doctor said, I don't have time and you know, I have no one else." Her voice trailed away. I pressed my hands to my mouth to suppress my cry. "Will you take care of the baby, Dev?"

Fear grabbed me as I stressed to listen to the answer but couldn't hear a thing, but before I could relax, she whispered, "thanks." Dev might have just nodded; losing his love must have been unbearable.

His love? Who was I then?

I tiptoed inside and stood at the edge of the door. Dev was sitting on a chair with his back to the door, hunched over, and holding her hand, with a baby sleeping beneath their entangled hands. Mehak... her skin was the fairest shade and her long, dark hair was sprawled over the bed. She looked beautiful even on the death bed.

The monitor flashed with a straight line and a cry escaped my throat. Not at her demise, but the demise of what I once had with Dev.

"Avni!" Dev's face was pale when he turned back.

I ran outside, trying to muffle my cry.

"Avni, wait. Avni, please wait!" Dev's voice followed me, but he didn't. Of course, he had his priorities, and I wasn't one of them. I ran away, and I kept on running like a fanatic, ignoring the judgemental stares of passers-by, wiping away my tears all the way to my home. What did I feel throughout the long, suffocating moments? Betrayed? That word failed to do justice to what I felt. I felt robbed. Robbed of trust, of love, of faith, of hope. Robbed of the long years of our marriage, of a hundred thousand things that couldn't be conveyed in words. And after being robbed of it all, I felt hollow. Yes, hollow, the word did enough justice to what I felt. I ran up to my home, but I couldn't make it to my bedroom. Tired and broken, I stumbled down in our living room, curling into a ball, trembling and crying.

It was around midnight Dev returned with their baby.

She should have been our baby.

What followed was ugly as I started throwing things, and screaming and shouting, losing all control. Dev placed the baby on the side diwan and reached me. His confrontation that it was a mistake, and he didn't love Mehak, fell on deaf ears. Though, I knew Dev was not lying because I had heard their conversation, but did it matter? Especially with living proof of their union in our house? He cheated me, he betrayed me. That was the truth.

I hated him when he said I wasn't reachable and that's why he turned to Mehak, and it was only once, but I didn't trust him anymore. He was suddenly a stranger, a stranger who had a daughter, a love, a life I knew nothing about. I spent years in the same home, same room, same bed with a man I knew nothing about. He was not my husband; he was a stranger. I was gasping for breath. I needed help. I needed Dev. Why was

I expecting help from the man who had pushed me into that bottomless pit? Why was hope such a weak thing?

He hesitantly held me and I let him. I should have pushed him away, but I crumbled into his arms as if his touch would make me feel secure again, unite me with the man who wasn't a stranger, who was the man I had loved and trusted.

"Mehak... I..." then there was a long pause, a loaded silence, death of a heart, "I mean... Avni,"

I pushed him away, and we stood apart, my eyes rooted to his face, his bloodshot eye wandering everywhere, but my face.

The silence between us was darker than the sky outside. It was pierced with a baby's cry. I prepared myself to look at her, but all the strength I had assumed melted away when I saw her.

She was fair and beautiful... just like her mother.

Dev hesitantly lifted the baby in his arms, and the wail that left me then didn't feel like my own. It might have echoed around the town.

"Avni, please stop!" He kept her back on the bed, and it was difficult to say who had more tears amongst the two of us.

"Really? Is it only my business to stop? Why couldn't you stop when you were fucking her?" I screamed, throwing everything I could get my hands on.

"Avni... I am sorry." He held my hand mid-air and held me tight and, despite wanting to push him away, I melted in his arms and cried. But soon, an image flashed before me. It was not me, it was Mehak he was consoling, it was her he was kissing on the forehead, it was her... it was her... it wasn't me. And finally, I got the strength to push him away.

"Just leave!" I whispered, though I wanted him to stay and console me. A look of defeat clouded his face, and he eyed the baby with a torn look. He was hurting, but I was damaged. There was a huge difference. Hesitantly, he walked out and I let the baby cry for a long time. That was the only way I could

hurt him. But after hours, when my anger finally subsided, and I looked at the little girl who had finally slept hungry, her thumb in her mouth, I realized what a bitch I had become.

The next day onwards, though I enjoyed hurting Dev, I couldn't carry the guilt of hurting the child. Whenever she cried, I immediately gave her the milk bottle. Even with a full stomach, she cried sometimes. Dev would just pace in the room outside, but he didn't dare to enter. I couldn't decide if I was happy to see him in pain or if I was sad at what I had become. But I would take her in my arms and cuddle her.

My arms were filled with the soft, tender touch of a child, the touch I had craved for, longed for, prayed for. What pained me the most wasn't the fact that it was not my child, it was that it was Dev's child. The pain of being childless was now mine alone.

As I cradled her in my arms for hours, whenever a flicker of motherhood stirred in me, I kept her back on the bed, stared at her innocent face away from all the worries, unaware of the realities of life. And sometimes I just hated it. I just couldn't figure out how anyone in the world could hate such an adorable sight. Maybe the mother inside me had died long back and what happened in the last few days was just like stabbing a dead body. Sometimes I would cry for hours, sometimes I would just sit still, watching nothing in particular, but Tia's cries often came as a rescue to alter my thoughts.

What started as a duty soon became a routine. And slowly I accepted her as a part of my life. She was my duty; God had chosen me to take care of her, so be it. And I started carrying out my responsibilities without bickering with Dev. But it was just my duty, I often told myself. Not that I loved her, anyway; I constantly reminded myself of who she was.

But whenever she crawled and lay on my chest, the long-dead motherhood breathed, even if only for a second, and when *she kissed my cheeks, I was tempted to kiss her back. It took me all the effort in the world to not kiss her back and every time my willpower succeeded; a strange void filled me.*

I was a perfect caretaker, but it didn't give me any pleasure or pride.

Because imperfect things done out of love are far better than perfect things done out of duty.

***

A noise pulled me to present, and the light from Dev's room, across from mine, pierced the dead dark of my own room. He must have opened his laptop and started working. It was three in the night, and like me he couldn't sleep, but unlike me he had options to divert his mind.

CHAPTER THIRTY-NINE

AVNI

I was setting the table for lunch when I received a call from my mom. After regular pleasantries and asking after everyone's wellbeing, she asked me, "Don't you ever miss us, your parents?" Her voice was weak and tired.

"What kind of question is that?" I said into the Bluetooth, bringing plates from the kitchen.

"Do you even remember the last time you came home? It's been more than eight years. Eight years." She stressed the timeline. "We can't always fly down to see you."

After getting married and moving to Dubai, I visited home only once. The past had pounded on me, like a hungry tiger waiting in the bushes for its prey, and it had ripped me apart when it caught me. I decided to never return.

"Avni, are you listening?" her voice pierced through my thoughts.

"Yes mom, but Dev is too busy with his work and..." I sat down on the chair, finally. With this conversation, I couldn't focus on anything else.

"But you and Tia can come. I am sure Dev won't mind. *Beta*, we are getting old. God knows when the call will come."

"Mom, please don't say that," I murmured. 'You are all that I have,' I wanted to add but didn't.

"Your dad is not keeping well and he keeps on asking me when you will come to meet us. Please discuss with Dev and plan something." Dad is no more the man who used to hit his wife. Everything changed after I tried to commit suicide. Pain changes everything.

"Okay, mom."

Mostly, my parents visited me every two to three years, and I waited all the time for those few weeks we spent together. Mom had been pleading with me to see her for a while now, but the mere thought of going back to India scared me. The force of memories was too strong, but today the shiver in mom's voice hit me hard.

In the evening, when I discussed it with Dev, as expected he said that he had some important business meetings so he wouldn't be able to join us, but that Tia and I could go. Or I could go alone, leaving Tia. His sentence hit me hard but I said I would take Tia with me. After hearing numerous horrifying stories of harassment by caretakers, I couldn't leave Tia with one. My parents didn't know much about Tia's identity. I just told them that I adopted a girl child and they were happy for me.

This was the only benefit of living in a far-off land—you could hide the ugly parts of your life from your parents and show them a rosy picture.

The doorbell rang and Tia ran to open the door. Dev's parents were standing at the door, shouting, 'Surprise!' and Tia started dancing with excitement. Dev's mother lifted Tia in her arms, kissed her, and gave her a chocolate.

"How long will you stay, grandma?" Tia asked and she replied, "five days". Tia tried to convince them to stay longer, but they had some important work to finish after that.

We told them the same lie about Tia that we told to my parents. And every time my parents or Dev's parents visited, we behaved like a normal couple, laughed and talked like a normal family, even slept in the same room, on the same bed, with Tia between us.

Between us.

Tearing us apart, the way she did when she came into existence. I stared into Dev's face late in the night when he was asleep in the same bed and I tried to recognize him. He still felt like a known stranger. I was tempted to ruffle his hair as I did in the past, but the image of the hospital flashed in front of my eyes and I pulled back. Why Dev? Why did you do this to me? The question that constantly haunted me was: what if she was still alive? Would he have tried to include me in his family or simply walked out of my life? He had told me a thousand times that he would never have left me, and when I asked him what he would have done about his illegit family he never had any answer. I wanted to hear a confident "Yes, I would have left them." I might be mean to want it but I wanted to hear that desperately. Sometimes he meekly spelled out those golden words but I knew he lied. There was no use of imaginary questions and imaginary answers, so I grew out of them over time.

Each night I slept with him, a whirlwind of emotions passed through me. Every night I stared into his face, I found something new. On some days it was a flock of grey on the sides of his hair, on some days it was the new wrinkle on his forehead, on some days I noticed the tanning on his face had deepened. Sometimes I noticed he looked sad even when he was asleep. Was he turning from a known stranger into an unknown stranger?

CHAPTER FORTY

AVNI

I was reading a book when Dev's name flashed on my mobile.

"Avni, your tickets are booked for the 24th of next month."

"Okay."

Sometimes I yearned to have a longer conversation. I wanted to ask him whether he had his lunch or not. But no matter how hard I tried, I failed. I knew a simple hint from my end would melt some barriers. Things wouldn't change overnight but it could be a new beginning, but I just couldn't forgive his betrayal. How could I, when his betrayal was growing day by day in front of my own eyes? How could I forgive Dev's betrayal as long as Tia was with us? And her presence in our life was forever.

Unaware of all my thoughts, Tia jumped on me.

"Mumma, why are you so sad. Are you ill?" She touched my forehead and guilt brushed through me. She was just six years old, but she was always worried about me.

I was about to hug her back when a thought crossed my mind...like always. Was she like her mother? And my hands stopped midway.

"No, Tia, I am fine." I freed myself from her hug. "Did you finish your homework?"

"Yes, mummy" she again jumped on my lap, totally ignorant of my hint. "Mumma tell me, what happened? Why are you so sad?"

"Nothing, Tia" I pulled her down from my lap. "We are going to India next month and I was just planning what all needs to be done."

"We are going to India? To Nana Nani? Wow!" She started jumping in excitement.

"Mumma, pack my favorite pink dress, ok? And my Barbie too." And her chatter was on and I couldn't help but feel something for this little girl who was not my daughter. No, it wasn't love, but it wasn't hatred either.

Days turned into weeks and finally, after all the shopping was done and all the things to be taken were accumulated in one place, I opened my suitcase. I opened a gateway to my troubled emotions. India.

Sometimes I felt like I was out of that phase of my life completely, by mind, body, and soul. And yet sometimes, I felt my heart was left there and an empty exterior walked out of it.

I didn't want to, but I couldn't help but think of him.

I couldn't even speak his name to myself. I didn't even want to think of the reason.

On a beautiful day, he entered my life with a splash of colors. We turned from strangers to friends and then from friends to lovers. Even the thought of departure was unbearable, but then time changed it all. We turned from lovers to...to...I didn't know. Friends, enemies, strangers? Nothing could precisely define that relation...it was nameless.

My heart was broken into a thousand pieces and they say time heals everything. Yes, it healed me too, but an important piece was lost somewhere in the labyrinth of time. Nonetheless, love found me again, I found love again and life continued at a steady pace as if nothing changed. Like a torn-out chapter of a story, the memories of my first love faded, changing nothing in my life.

But then someday a silent tear flowed, a secret smile enveloped my lips. I smiled at an image that's wasn't real, wasn't imaginary. A feeling of a deep loss enveloped me. Why?

The secret remained somewhere in those torn chapters of my life.

CHAPTER FORTY-ONE

AVNI

The plane landed in India. An overwhelming sensation washed over me as I stepped down. The moment my feet touched the ground, I realized I had never left this place. A string of memories, fragile yet strong, tied me to this place. And now, when I was here, my legs gave away and I stumbled back at the exit of the airport.

"What happened, Mumma?" Tia asked holding my hand.

"Nothing," I said, suddenly feeling so tired that it was taking effort even to speak. I shook my head when a man in the distance offered to help.

"You look sad again." Tia tilted her head.

"No Tia. I am fine."

"Are you not happy to see your mummy and daddy?"

"Of course, I am. Just that I am tired."

"Will she hug you when you meet her?" she asked, tilting her head and hugging herself.

"What kind of question is that?"

"Mumma, please tell," she said, gripping the handles of her bag, slung on her shoulders.

"Yes."

"Will she kiss you too?" she pouted.

"Of course, she will?" I said with a hint of irritation. "Come, let's move. We are getting late." I forced myself to get into action.

When I saw my parents, guilt swept over me. I should have visited them more often. They had aged beyond their age. The wrinkles were deeper and highlighted the loneliness in their tired eyes. Dad looked particularly worn-out and thinner than the last time. But as soon as they saw us, their eyes glinted with life.

Mom ran up to me and hugged me tightly, and a teardrop landed on my shoulder. When she hugged Tia, Tia hugged my mother back with all the strength she had. It was a while before she loosened her grip. She chuckled when dad gave her a chocolate and kissed her on the forehead.

Soon we reached home. I was standing at the front door but in my mind, I was running. I was running hard from the memories that were chasing me. I slowly entered the house after eight long -years and I was so tired that I stopped running in my mind, and finally, the memories got hold of me and they devoured me like a hungry predator waiting for its prey.

Avinash smiled from the photo hanging in the drawing-room. This photo was shot six months before he left us. He was wearing a white kurta and his eyes spoke from the photo. I had teased him that mom should send this photo to his prospective brides when the hunt starts, little did I know this photo would hang on the wall with a garland. I pulled the garland from the photo. "How many times have I told you not to put a garland on his photo?" I rushed upstairs before I would lose it.

My mind warned me, but my heart pushed me towards his room. With trembling hands, I pushed the door of his room, but I didn't enter. I couldn't. Not because my mind warned me anymore; it had shut down totally. My legs jammed and my eyes were focused on his bed.

Empty bed.

This bed should not have been empty, it should have been crowded with his family - his wife and kids. With that thought my pain became physical. A severe aching shot through my chest and I sat down involuntarily on the floor. His words echoed in the dead silence.

Hey bro.

Blunder queen.

I will leave you forever.

Those last words always hit me the hardest and reminded me I was the reason for his...

Death.

How strange, that we were afraid of using the obvious word! I ached to hug him one last time, tell him how sorry I was, tell him he never suffocated me. I loved his protectiveness, and I loved it, even more, when I lost it. I was rocking back and forth when a small hand landed on my shoulder.

"Mumma!" Tia was staring at me wide-eyed and I noticed I was trembling all over. Her eyes reflected fear. She didn't ask me what happened to me as she always did, but she was staring at me. I covered my face in my palms and her small arms came around me. I might have hugged her back because I just wanted to hold on to something. Anything. But my hands were locked on my face in between her hug.

"Mumma, please don't cry," she said with a wobbly voice.

After a while, I forced out the words, "I am fine, Tia. Let's go down. Nani must be waiting for us for dinner." She left me reluctantly and we walked downstairs.

Tia was quiet for a long time, but strangely, today I wanted her to chatter to divert my mind. She only needed a little nudge from mom and her chattering was on. Thankfully, with all the talking Tia did, my mind couldn't dwell on the past as much as I had worried.

After a few days, dad got a call informing him of the demise of his childhood friend. Dad was adamant to go for his last rituals in the other town. Given his heart problems, the doctors denied him to travel alone.

Mom and I were removing peas from the pods. I looked at dad who was silently staring out of the window. He had mellowed down and was forever guilty that he couldn't give us a happy childhood. Looking at him, I couldn't even remember the man who used to...NO. I didn't want to go there. "Mom. I think we should let him go. You can accompany him."

Mom stopped working on the peas. "I can't, Avni. You have visited us after so many years."

"It's ok mom, it's just a matter of a day."

Mom wasn't convinced but when she looked at dad, she agreed hesitantly.

"Are you sure you can manage alone?" She stared back at me.

"Yes, mom."

She thought for a while and said, "We will be back by tomorrow evening, But...do you really think..."

"Mom," I held her hand. "I will be fine." She nodded and walked up to dad.

They left by the afternoon and suddenly, all the strength I had assumed I had, left the home with them.

CHAPTER FORTY-TWO

AVNI

Painful memories are like quicksand—the harder you fight to swim out, the deeper you drown.

I needed to step out of the house to breathe. "You want to go out?" I asked Tia.

"Out for fun? Yay!"

She started dancing on the bed. "I will wear my favorite pink frock. You packed it. Right?"

I nodded and got her ready. Then I changed into my churidar as fast as I could and we rushed out.

Soon the cab arrived, and we got into it. Stepping out of home had never been such a relief. I tried to focus on the surroundings that had changed drastically—the huge garden was replaced by a big mall, there were fewer trees and more buildings. And before I knew it, the cab passed by his studio. I closed my eyes. No, I couldn't gather the courage to look at it. Some emotions are better buried. The moment you free them they enslave you.

But closing my eyes didn't help much. He just got closer with my eyes closed, staring at me like no one ever did, like I was precious. His strong arms stretched out to take me in and I ached to step back in my past, in his arms, where I learned what love was. Whenever I thought of him, a particular moment knocked at the door of my memories, the moment when my emotions were at its peak, the moment when he confessed his love, the moment when his guards broke down and he allowed me to see his scars. His deep eyes had seen so much in life yet reflected faith. Did I take away that faith from him? Maybe I did, but what option did I have? Being with him meant being constantly reminded of the guilt that could have drowned me...and then him.

"Mumma, why are you crying again?" Tia's soft voice pulled me out of my memories.

The cab driver's curious face on the rear-view mirror embarrassed me. I chose not to reply in my choked voice. Tia was, after all, used to not receive a reply when I was too stressed out.

After a while, when the cab waited at a crossroad for the signal to turn green, Tia shouted, "Mumma see that cute doll? I want it!"

I replied without looking at the doll she was pointing to, "we will get a doll from the mall."

"But Mumma, I want that doll only. She is so chubby. In the mall, we get those skinny dolls. Please, please, please, Mumma."

I looked in the direction she was pointing. It was an overcrowded place with a small toy shop at the end of the road with a few toys arranged on shelves outside the shop.

"Mumma please, Mumma please." She pulled my hand. I freed my hand from her grip and nodded.

I told the cab driver to drop us at the shop and purchased the doll for Tia. After walking out of the shop, I was about to call a rickshaw when someone tapped on my shoulder.

Avni? She asked me when I turned to face her.

"Priyanka?" I exclaimed.

"Oh my God, Avni." She put her palms on her mouth. "You have changed so much! I wasn't sure it was you.

"Even you have changed a lot," I smiled.

"Yeah, with all these tyres!" she held her stomach and grimaced.

"No, no, I didn't mean that."

"But look at you! Are you getting younger?" she eyed me from top to bottom. "You haven't put on a single kilo. And turn around."

She shoved my shoulder, so my back was to her.

"When did you get that long hair? You don't look like that messy girl anymore."

"Messy?" I grimaced turning back to her.

She bit her lips. "Oops! Sorry, I didn't mean that."

Before I could reply, she said, "Hey cutie," She waved at Tia who was standing behind me. "Like mother like daughter," she said, and I felt something heavy in my chest. No, she wasn't like me. Her skin was fairer than mine, her hazel eyes were not at all like my brown eyes. Her features were way sharper than mine. She was like...

"She looks like her dad?" Priyanka said, looking closely at Tia.

She confirmed that Tia didn't look like me.

I nodded, forcing a smile.

"My daughter is almost her age too..." And once she started chattering, Priyanka didn't stop. It was almost after fifteen minutes that she exclaimed, "Oh my God! I was on my way to pick up my daughter from her tuition. I am late. I need to go. Are you going to stay for some time?"

"Yeah."

"Ok, I will catch up with you soon. Bye!" she said and walked away. I looked at her until she vanished into the crowd.

"Tia, come, let's..." I turned back but Tia was not there. My first reaction was irritation. Why couldn't she stand still? But when I looked around and couldn't see her anywhere, my irritation turned into panic.

I walked to the toy shop, but she wasn't there. I asked the shopkeeper, but he knew nothing. I walked out, calling her name. Before I realized it, I was shouting her name, running frantically here and there, showing her photo on my mobile to passersby, but nobody had seen her. I was showing her photo to a stranger when a small boy in ragged clothes walked up to me and gave me a piece of paper. I looked at the paper and then at him. With trembling hands, I opened the note.

"Your daughter is with me. Don't you dare inform anyone if you want to see her alive. Walk back to your home silently. I will contact you."

Dread twisted in my gut, and by the time I looked up the boy was gone. I looked around sweating with fear; the tall dark man around the corner—was he the one? The plump man staring at me from the tyre puncture stall—could he be the one? The shopkeeper where I got the doll...could he? Suddenly, all the faces turned dangerous and each step I took was burdened with fear and anxiety. Finally, when I reached the rickshaw stand, I couldn't speak.

"Where to, madam? The rickshaw driver asked when I got into the rickshaw.

"A...Akota." I forced out the word. I kept looking around me to find the kidnapper, to find Tia, but all the faces had blurred behind the anxiety that was consuming me.

Opening the lock with my trembling hands took me three attempts. My legs gave way as soon as I entered the room and I crumbled on the floor. The switchboard was at a distance and seemed unreachable. The phone ring sounded so loud in the dead silence that it startled me. God, I couldn't even open the purse, my hands were trembling so hard! Finally, when I pulled out my mobile from the purse, Dev's name flashed on it.

Panic surged through me. What would I tell him? I lost Tia? Just like that? Would he even trust me? Would he doubt some foul play? No, he wouldn't. Or would he? I didn't pick up the phone and thankfully Dev didn't call again. It was a while before my breathing got even, and I reached for the light switch to turn on the lights. I slowly walked up to the kitchen and gulped down a glass of water in a single breath.

A knock at the door almost made me scream. I ran to the door and then stopped, took one deep breath, and opened the door. I stepped out and there was no one, but there was a letter on the veranda. I picked it up and stumbled back inside. "Come to the backside of SDU College ALONE. If you want to see your daughter alive, don't dare to call the police or inform anyone else. At 10 PM sharp."

How did he know my home? Did he follow my rickshaw? Could I have caught him if I was more attentive? I vaguely remembered my mother telling me about increased kidnapping cases in the area, and how the child was returned safely if the kidnappers' demands were met. I took a few deep breaths to steady my uneven breathing and glanced at the clock. It was just 7 p.m. How was I going to spend three long hours? I needed to focus. Think of anything to avoid the panic attack from conquering me.

Tia's bag. A small pink bag with Barbie printed over it. It was on the open rack beside my bed. She had packed it herself when we left. I never bothered to check what she packed, what she thought about, how she felt.

I pulled her bag to the bed and then I opened the zipper. One by one I took out her things—her favorite white teddy, a colorful hanky, a Barbie doll, and a diary.

I opened the first page of the diary.

"Tia's Diary," it read.

I vaguely remembered that she had told me she was a writer and that she wrote stories. I turned the page.

The new story of Cindrelllaa.

There was a cutee girl who lived with her mumaa papa.

Mumaa and papa luvd he soo mucch.

Mumaa hug her tite when she returnd frm skool.

"Will she hug you when you meet her?" She had asked at the airport and when mom hugged her, she had held on to her for so long. She knew she won't get another hug.

Mumaa give her a good night kiss.

"Will she also kiss you?" She had asked with a longing in her eyes. At that moment, she didn't look like the girl who chatted nonstop. She looked like a girl who was never kissed.

"Mumaa was haappy. With her."

Mumma, why are you sad?

Papa takes little Cindrelllaa for a ride.

Mumma, Manisha was teasing me that her papa takes her for a ride daily.

A drop of tear descended from my eyes on her notebook, smearing her words. And then it all came out. I cried, hugging the diary close to my heart. And it hit me that it wasn't the fear of Dev's reaction, it was the fear of losing Tia that was killing me. It was the emptiness of my bed and my heart, the absence of her soft little hands covering my waist. The silence created a stark contrast with her never-ending chatter and reminded me of the reason for the silent tears flowing down my cheeks. I remembered the pang I felt in my heart when I first saw her innocence. The way her soft little fingers bound around my finger and how much I loved that gesture and how much I hated myself for it.

Always longing for a hug, a kiss, and some love from us, did she expect too much? My behavior in the initial days of her arrival had even scared Dev so much that he never spent much time with Tia. He was always busy with his work and at home, he was always tired. He avoided Tia like a plague, but there was longing in his eyes. What had I become? I was so overwhelmed with my grief that I failed to see the grief of the people around me, especially Tia, a little girl who, at her age, shouldn't even know what grief was.

On a normal day, she would have slept by now. I would have removed her soft tiny hands from my waist and turned my back to her. Now, when she was not there to hug me, when she was not curled up in my bed, I hugged her Barbie doll and kissed it nonstop, regretting every moment I had pushed her away. The next three hours were the longest three hours of my life.

Then it was time to leave home, time to save Tia. I thought of calling mom and dad to inform them, but dad might not be able to handle any stress. The doctor had warned us to keep him away from stress. Still, I wrote a note and kept it beside dad's pillow. I mentioned that if I went missing, they should start searching behind SDU College.

I walked down to the place. On my way, there was a big hoarding in which a mother was hugging her daughter and they were both laughing, and suddenly an image emerged in front of me—an imaginary image of me and Tia. Tia was smiling in my arms and we were happy.

Happy.

I felt a knot in my chest. The pain overwhelmed me. It was the same pain.

The same pain of losing a child.

CHAPTER FORTY-THREE

AVNI

The street lights illuminated the college gate. On any other day, it would have brought hundreds of memories, but not today. I was too tired to even think about the past. I stared around but there was no one around. The streets were deserted at this time of the night and my body went cold with dread.

There was a piece of paper near the gate, kept beneath a big stone, and I opened it. "Come inside."

It was dark inside. I second guessed my decision of walking alone without any help, but now it was late. I couldn't turn back, I couldn't put Tia's life at risk. I climbed on the gate and jumped inside.

"Tia!" My voice echoed in the silence. Apart from the sound of the cool breeze, the only sound was of me walking on dried leaves.

I hesitated, but only for a moment. I needed to keep walking. The thought of Tia in this place with a stranger sucked the life out of me. I tried to stay alert amid all the turmoil going on in my mind.

A scream escaped my throat when a shadow lurked behind a tree. Before I could protest, the shadow jumped at me and a strong hand covered my mouth and lifted me, pulling me in the dark. I struggled to get free of his grasp, but his arms were too strong against my fragile body, and after pulling me inside to an area dimly lit by the light inside the premises, totally cut off from the outside world, he left me.

I turned around.

And the world stopped.

All the thoughts clouding my mind came to a halt. The whisper of the breeze was drowned in a silence so deep that my breathing became audible.

"Vivaan!" I barely managed to speak.

In those hollow, numb moments when my memories cheated me, holding back pieces of precious moments, pushing just broken pieces towards me, I wondered if those pieces were real or just a reflection of my desires. But seeing him in front of me broke the façade. It was real. The love. The hatred. The closeness. The loss. And the unbearable pain. It was all real.

He looked...different. A strange roughness had been added to his skin, accentuated by the slight stubble on his chin. His hair was shorter, highlighting the sharp angles of his face that didn't retain a single boyish hue of the boy I had known. Now he was all man, oozing confidence and power, with a hint of severity. But when I looked into his eyes...he was still the same. The rawness I had fallen in love with was still there, and it still had the power to make my heart beat wild, but there was something new in his eyes too.

Revenge.

I loved him, I hated him but I never feared him.

Until now.
What did he see in me? The broken promise?
Or the broken girl behind the broken promise?

CHAPTER FORTY-FOUR

VIVAAN

Her hair had grown just like the way they did in my paintings, an inch in a year. What precise calculation! Only, they had curled at the end, adding to the allure. I remembered how soft they felt and fought the urge to touch them again. A big maroon bindi adorned her forehead. Her dark eyes were as captivating as I remembered them to be, but something had changed. Why did it make me sad? Her lips reminded me of the taste of...I didn't want to go there.

"So, you remember my name?" I added as much sarcasm to my voice as possible, my eyes refusing to leave her face.

She took a moment to find her voice, but when she did find it, she avoided my question. "Where is Tia?"

The same husky voice.

"Please tell me where Tia is."

She still twitched her fingers when nervous.

"See, this is between you and me. Do you want revenge? I am here to face it. But please leave my daughter."

She still put her family before herself.

While her mind wandered between a thousand questions, my mind was busy just observing her. It's been ten years. Ten years!

"Are you listening? Where is Tia?" She raised her voice, looking around in panic.

"So worried about your child?" I reminded myself I didn't call her here just to see her, though I could spend the whole night just staring at her.

I had seen love in those big eyes and even hatred, but this fear was an alien feeling and I wasn't sure whether I liked it or not.

An announcement made by a patrolling police jeep pierced through my trance. "Riots have broken in the city and curfew has been imposed. Please don't leave your homes. Stay alert. Stay safe."

"Come inside where no one can see us," I said. Fear was written all over her face, but her daughter was with me, so she had no option but to follow me. I led her to the place where we used to meet in those days—the secluded porch. The place, just like me had been unable to catch up with the fast-moving world. It was still the same, unattended, wild, and yet barren in a strange way. The moonlight lighted the place generously and the little white flowers shone in midst of the weeds.

The last time I visited this porch was a few days back. In the initial phase of our break-up, I used to visit this place daily. But with time, days turned to weeks and weeks to months and months to years.

The little sapling of our love had turned into a gigantic tree. Its branches were touching the sky. Looking at the strength of that tree, I wondered if relationships were like trees—you needed to put in a lot of effort in the beginning, but once its roots were strong nothing could stop that love from growing, not even loss or betrayal or the pain that came with it. On second thought, I wasn't sure love was like that tree. Why was I always confused when it came to love?

For a long time, we both glanced at that tree. When our eyes met, I found a forgotten longing in her eyes. Distant sounds of hope and laughter rang in the air. She slumped down on the porch involuntarily and before her body could slump further, she held on to a creeper rounding around the pillar. "Where is my Tia?" She barely managed to speak.

"So much pain for your child?"

"Please tell me where she is," she repeated tiredly.

"I am loving this...this fear!" I paused, drew in a sharp breath. "This pain of losing a child."

"Losing a child?" she gasped and jumped to her feet, "What did you do to her? I will kill you if you did anything to harm her?" She screamed, her hands curling into a fist, "where is Tia?" She stared at the sky and screamed again, "where is she?"

"What do you think?" The calmness of my voice was a blunt contrast to her screams.

"Vivaan!" she said as if my name was no more familiar on her lips. "Please!"

"So much love for your child?" My voice lowered and rose in an instant. "Then why did you kill my child Avni? Why did you kill *our* child?"

Suddenly the air became thick and the words dangled in the air, defying the law of nature. It echoed senselessly, maybe only in my mind. But in her too.

Her eyes reflected a thousand emotions, pain dominating it all. And a question: I knew? Yes, I knew. Now when the truth was spoken aloud, the past came alive and everything replayed in my mind.

The news of Avni's suicidal attempt had snatched the earth beneath my legs. I daily visited the hospital until she recovered, but her dad never allowed me to see her.

Long after she recovered and left the place, I got to know from the doctor who turned out to be a relative of Arjun that Avni had aborted a child and maybe the news of the pregnancy was the reason she tried to commit suicide.

Yes, I knew, my baby had been killed. I closed my eyes but before I could drift away a loud thud startled me. When I opened my eyes Avni was on the floor, curled into a ball, gasping to breathe, and trembling heavily.

Shit. She had a panic attack.

"Avni, Avni sit straight and take a deep breath." I rushed to her, lifted her by her shoulders, and helped her sit. Her earthy aroma captured my senses and it was becoming hard to keep the distance, fighting the urge to protect her, embrace her in my arms. I helped her sit against the pillar and rushed to the nearby tap. I got some water in my palms and sprinkled some on her face. I rushed to the tap again and got some water for her to drink. She pushed aside my hand.

"Avni, you need to calm down. You are here for Tia." Thankfully, I knew how to convince her.

She sipped the water and as her soft lips brushed my palms, a thousand desires were unchained. It took the last ounce of my willpower to control my urge to hug her tightly and kiss away her worries like the old days. She soon pulled back and rested her back on the pillar, creating distance between us. Once again.

I stood up and walked back to get a grip on my emotions. I pushed my hands, which were still burning from her touch, in my pocket.

CHAPTER FORTY-FIVE

VIVAAN

When her breathing calmed down, she got up and the first thing she asked was, "please tell me where Tia is." She still avoided talking about the child she had aborted. What the fuck?

"Why do you think I called you here?" I stared hard at her. I was losing my patience. I waited for a decade to get answers to the questions that didn't let me sleep peacefully for a single night. And she wanted her answer so soon? No way.

"Why did you kill my child, Avni?" I paused "Our child. Why?" Yes, I wanted to hurt her when I grabbed her arm tightly, but this hurt was nowhere near the hurt she gave me.

She jerked my hand away. "What else I could have done?"

"I could have raised the baby if you were so keen to get rid of it!"

"You can never understand the shame I went through. My parents were not yet out of the pain of losing Avinash! I couldn't humiliate them any further by becoming an unmarried mother."

"Unmarried?" I paused. Inhaled. Exhaled. "We could have married." And with those words, I drifted to the time it was still a possibility. I closed my eyes to cut off from this world, from the girl standing in front of me who broke my heart into a thousand pieces.

"It wasn't as easy as you think." Her whisper barely made it to me; my eyes were still closed.

"Hell! And it was easy to wipe out the child, kill the baby?" I shouted, staring at her.

"No, no, no! It wasn't easy!" She shook her head frantically, her hands in the air. "It wasn't easy, it wasn't!" Her voice dropped every time she repeated the words.

"I never shared my life with anyone the way I did with you, Avni." I pointed a finger at her, not so much in accusation as in regret. "You know, even after getting a family the feeling of abandonment never left me. Dad says our destiny is in our hands. My mother left me, leaving me with a thousand questions. I couldn't do a thing about it. As I grew up and got a grip on my life, I promised myself I would protect my child from the slightest scratch. And yet my child was wiped off without my knowledge. What the hell is in my hand then?" My hand hurt when I punched the pillar, but somehow it felt good. "You might not remember the thing I never forgot. I told you once, 'my child will never feel unwanted, unloved.'" Back then, I had said 'our child'but now those words felt hollow, somehow wrong too, yet I had already used them once. I punched the wall again. "I just want an answer from you. Why? Why did you do it? Did your hatred for me took over all the goodness in you? Yes, I made a mistake, but did I intentionally kill Avinash?" Her eyes moistened at his name, but I couldn't care less. "Yes, I made a mistake, and I hated myself for it as long as I could, but my mistake was not as severe as the punishment you decided for me. I just hate you. I hate you!" And with those words a weight lifted off me. Long back, she had said the same words at the same place and left me yearning for her. But now, years later, as I uttered those words, I realized it was not the truth. It was not a lie either. It dangled somewhere in between.

"Stop it!" she raised her hand in the air, "for God's sake, stop it! I know I am awful. I made a mistake and believe me, I never forgave myself. Yes, you are right. I was a bad mother but God has punished me enough for my sin. Please don't make it worse for me." Her voice trailed off at the last word.

"God has punished you enough?" I pointed at her in question. "You are living a happily married life, with a daughter who considers you the best mom in the world. All the fairy tales she has told me gives me an idea of your wonderful life and you tell me that God has punished you?"

"Fairy tales," she whispered. "Best mother in the world?" She said to herself, I guess. "I didn't give birth to her." Those words barely traveled to me. There was a distant look in her eyes. "I didn't give birth to her," she repeated. "I could never conceive again. Everyone must pay for their sins. I did too."

"She isn't your daughter?" Where was this going?

"I said I didn't give birth to her." She didn't give birth to Tia, but she was her daughter. She was still the same girl who loved unconditionally. It's just that I wasn't lucky enough to claim her love.

"You adopted her?" my voice dropped.

"No." Her tone suddenly changed and she turned her back to me. "She is the illegitimate daughter of my husband."

The words didn't disperse immediately, they hung in the silence that was...just sad.

She turned to look at me. "So, does that makes you happy?"

"Avni!" I breathed.

"What? You wanted me to be unhappy because I betrayed you. I told you I *am* unhappy. I am in as much pain as you are, or maybe even more. Now I guess you got your answer. I had sinned and I was supposed to be punished. Okay. God has punished me enough. So, can you please give me Tia back? Harming her would do no good to you. It can't satisfy your revenge."

"You think I can harm Tia?" My voice lost the harsh tone I had tried hard to hang on to. I hope I didn't sound as hurt as I was.

"No," she said sarcastically. "You kidnapped her and...and..." she gestured her hands in question, "God knows hid her where? You called me to a secluded place in the middle of the night and I should think that you can't harm her or that you can't harm me. For God's sake, Vivaan! Tell me if she is safe or not? Do you want to kill me? Come on, kill me." She walked up to me, lifted my hands, and wrapped them around her neck. "Kill me if that satisfies your urge for revenge, but leave Tia alone. For God's sake, spare her."

Her cold hands were wrapped around my palms and my palms were wrapped around her neck. How could I even stop my heart from beating so erratically? A decade earlier, she couldn't have stood so close to me without hugging or kissing me. Now, she had receded far away.

My hands were still on her neck and I couldn't maintain the sharp edge to my tone. It took me a while to find my voice. "I...I can never harm you Avni...or Tia." I averted my gaze from her face to the fallen leaves behind her.

I stepped back before my emotions consumed me. "I will send Tia to your place in the morning." I again pushed my hands in my pockets.

"Ok, then I should go," she said and turned around to leave.

"Avni, wait! It's risky out there."

"I can take care of myself. You don't need to worry about me." Her words pierced through me. I grabbed her arm and narrowed my glance at her. My voice was harsh but I didn't care, "you are not going anywhere. Do you understand that? If it is my presence that is unbearable, I will leave." I started to walk out.

"Vivaan, wait. I will stay."

She still worried for me. The fact was the only comfort in that tremulous night.

She sat on the porch and I stood behind, with my hands folded over my chest.

It was about midnight. The sound of crickets became prominent as the noises in my head began to fade. The air was loaded with the smell of night jasmine scattered on the grass. The moonlight that filtered through the branches of the trees, glinted on her face and the breeze caressed her long hair.

The calm breeze passed through us.

Us...

I wanted to paint that moment.

The porch and the weather opened a flood gate of memories. I remembered how we kissed each other endlessly on this same porch, I remembered the taste of her lips, the feel of her skin. One look at her and I knew the memories had hit us together.

She was still twitching her fingers. That meant she was still nervous. She diverted her gaze. That meant she didn't want me to read her. And, like me, she also struggled to keep her emotions in check. I didn't need to read her body language to know that.

God! We were meant to be together.

CHAPTER FORTY-SIX

VIVAAN

We needed to spend the night together. Talking was better than this uncomfortable silence.

"Tia loves you a lot," I said.

Her hands stopped playing with the grass blades. She looked glad that I spoke something and relieved that it wasn't about us.

"You are a great mom, Avni."

"I don't think so." She resumed her game with the grass blades.

"Why don't you?" I walked up to her and sat beside her, resting my hands on my knees, keeping enough distance between us to keep me sane. Her presence could make me insane even in the same city, let alone on the same porch.

"You can talk to me, Avni. You look tired. Not tired of the day but tired of life."

She glanced at me, and a sad smile enveloped her face. "From where should I start?" She picked up a night jasmine from the grass. "Tia," she said softly, "I have been mean to her. No, I never misbehaved with her. I was always a good caretaker." She looked thoughtful. "Yes, I was a good caretaker, but not a good mother."

"You were always a good mother, Avni. It's just that you didn't accept it."

"No, I failed her. Tia had this constant yearning for a mother's love but I failed to love her."

"You walked to this deserted place, risking your life. Only a mother can do that. The fear of losing her was written all over your face."

The smallest of smiles caressed her face but withered too soon. "I spoiled her childhood. I don't know if I missed the longing in her eyes or just ignored it."

"Longing?" I paused. "I agree she feels lonely. She was playing with her doll but then suddenly she asked, where is my Mumma? Do you think she must be missing me?"

Avni closed her eyes. "I missed her. I never thought I would, but I did." Her voice cracked. "I missed her as I've never missed anyone."

She opened her eyes and looked at me. "Thanks, Vivaan."

"Thanks?" I titled my head. "For what?

"For kidnapping Tia." She let out a feeble laugh. "I mean, for taking her away from me. It was only in her absence that I realized my love for her. The fear of losing her evoked feelings in me I had lost long back. I don't have the stretch marks or the memories of my child kicking in my stomach, but despite it all..." she tried not to cry, "I am a mother."

A mother.

I have seen her worrying for her mother, and then for her daughter, all from a distance. So much has changed in this period. The day she was broken due to her mother's pain I had hugged her. Now, when she was broken due to her daughter's pain, the few inches distance between us was unbreachable.

"I think it's time to forgive Dev too." Shit. Why couldn't I keep my mouth shut?

"You know his name?" she shot an exasperated look at me.

"Of course."

Hell, why was I failing to keep the conversation uncomplicated! I knew he was a computer engineer. 5'10", only child of his parents. I knew all about him and Avni until she vanished in a different land.

It was a while before she found her voice. "What makes you think I didn't forgive him."

"Well," I also pulled out a grass from the wilderness, because I couldn't look at her with this conversation. "Mom and dad were fighting over a silly issue at home, and Tia said, 'my Mumma and daddy never fight.'" I skipped the part how her words had burnt me with jealously. I also skipped the part about how I was scared that Tia might reveal her mother's name. I had lied at home that she was the daughter of a friend who was admitted to the hospital. Mom got suspicious of my story, but I had convinced her. "She had further said, 'because they never talk.'"

It was quiet for a while, before she uttered, "she is so observant. I never realized it."

"Is Dev a habitual cheater?" Shit! God, help me keep my mouth shut. I sat straighter, curing myself for the slip of my thoughts.

"No, no," she shook her head, "Dev is not like that. It was...a mistake."

The way her eyes glinted at Dev's name changed something inside me. This was the glint my name used to ignite in her. She had drifted far away. An image flashed in front of my eyes - an innocent girl dressed up like a boy, tripping flat on the floor amid a crowd. Two sweet dimples adorning her embarrassed face as she got up. No, I could never find her. She was lost.

The girl sitting next to me was not my Avni.

She was Dev's Avni.

At that moment, something receded far away from me. Maybe it was the love I once felt for this girl sitting next to me.

"You should also marry now." Her voice felt as if coming from a distance.

I couldn't respond for a while. A strange emptiness filled in the places where there had been love. And that was the whole of me.

She patiently waited for my response. She always did.

"How do you know I didn't marry?"

"Otherwise, your wife would have called you at least ten times. After all, you are with your ex-girlfriend." She bit her lips. "Oops! Sorry...I...I mean—"

"It's ok, blunder queen." I patted the back of her head.

And then we laughed. With tears in our eyes.

Then it was quiet for a while until she broke the silence, "but seriously, you should get married."

I looked at her and I knew I could never love anyone the way I loved her once.

I couldn't even love her that way anymore. That was a sad revelation.

But a face flashed in front of me.

Kangana.

The dusky beauty with big eyes. She was the only person who could make me laugh anymore. More than her beauty or wit, it was her smile that amazed me. It was the way that broad smile had managed to survive on her face after all that had happened to her—the way poverty claimed her parents, the way she managed to get where she was.

'Why are you always so angry?' She had asked me once and I chose not to reply. But I guess she knew. Isn't that why she told me yesterday, 'Two broken people can get along well.'

'Or turn each other's life hell,' I had replied.

But on second thought, turning each other's life into hell wasn't such a bad option. I wasn't sure till yesterday, but while sitting here with Avni, if Kangana's thoughts crossed my mind, I guess that meant something.

"What's her name?" Avni asked, and I realized I was smiling.

"Kangana." The expression on her face mirrored mine when she had spoken of Dev.

"Tell me something more about her."

"She is a disaster." I smiled. "My fellow journalist. She gets into the murkiest of cases and gets out clean. If it's not complicated, it's not for her."

Long back, sitting on the same porch, we had confessed our love for each other. And now a decade later, we were confessing our love for different people. It was the saddest talk I ever had with anyone. Long back each word spoken brought us closer, and today each word spoken...I won't say they separated us, but yes, they liberated us from each other. Not entirely, but maybe in bits and pieces, maybe enough so that we could get some space to breathe.

As the night progressed, we talked about people we had known. She told me she met Priyanka and how much she had changed. I told her about Arjun, who was working with a reputed firm and had two kids. His dad was in the best of health. I also told him about Shreyansh, who, after two broken engagements, had finally got married and had one daughter.

We talked for hours about our lives and our families.

The first ray of sun had kissed the earth and we were still as fresh as we could be.

"Kanha will drop Tia at your place in the afternoon. I think the curfew will be lifted by then." Kanha didn't know anything about Avni and he wasn't the kind to report everything to mom, so sending Kanha to drop Tia was the safest bet.

"Kanha? How can he...he is so small!" She placed her hand on her chest, "Oh, he must be a grown-up boy now. Is he still the same, chubby and cute?"

"Chubby? Not at all. He is tall and lean. 'A difficult child' is what mom calls him. Mom always says that I was so mature at his age and I tell mom not to compare us. But Kanha is cool with almost everything unless you try to tie him in norms. Mom often teases dad by saying rebel son of rebel dad."

"And how are your parents?" she asked.

I didn't know how to answer that.

"Dad is flourishing in his business and he still counsels. Mom is not in the best of her health. She had a major accident last year and she is still recovering. Avni, I can't tell you how scared I was of losing her. Like you just said, when you feared losing Tia you realized how much you loved her. The same thing happened to me. We almost lost her, but she survived."

It surprised me how I was still so comfortable sharing my life with her. It all came out naturally without any effort. I remembered how hard I had hugged mom when the doctor said she was out of danger. How the doctor warned me to go easy and mom had said, 'I will just get better with that hug, doctor. His love can never harm me.' And I had cried like a small baby, resting my head on her lap. I never searched for anyone else in her face after that.

Avni was staring at my face, waiting silently for me to gather my thoughts like she always did. She never wanted to just listen, she always wanted to understand. God, help me not to fall in love with her all over again. I wanted to tell her to stop staring at me like that, but when she flinched, I realized I was also staring at her.

She suddenly diverted her gaze to the grass, avoiding the evident awkwardness.

"How are your parents?" I broke the silence.

We heard an announcement that the curfew had been lifted. But it seemed Avni wasn't as keen to leave as she was in the night.

"Much older than their age. Dad is a different person now; he cares for mom. He seems forever guilty that he couldn't give us a happy childhood. Everything changed after my suicidal attempt, after what I wrote in the suicidal note." Her voice cracked. "I wrote," she swallowed the lump in her throat. "I wrote that I can't tolerate all the noises coming from their room without Avi..." her hand reached her throat and her voice broke with her next word, "Avinash." And it was back there, the raw pain of losing Avinash. In the past decade, Avni's memories never knocked alone, Avinash was always there with her. I mean, that's how inseparable they were. Avni wasn't the same without Avinash.

I pulled out the note from my pocket, that I had waited for so long to give her. "I got this letter in Avinash's tent when we packed up after our camping trip. Whatever happened there made me forget about it at the time. Years later, when I was cleaning my bag, I got it. It's a letter from Avinash." The letter wasn't in an envelope and I had breached their privacy, but I couldn't help it. And I had cried after reading it.

I bent a little, so she could reach out to the letter. Her hands trembled as she touched it. The way she stared at the letter; I knew she wasn't ready to read it yet.

And once the first tear broke free, there was no stopping.

Some things were not right or wrong. They just were. It was pure. It was sinful. It was happy. It was sad. It was so much that I couldn't say what it was but...I just couldn't control myself. I hugged her, probably for the last time. After a moment of hesitation, her arms came around me with the same ferocity. Even after a decade, when everything had changed, her embrace filled with me the familiar comfort I felt in those days and the pain of losing her once again ripped me apart. Neither of us tried to stop the tears flowing one after the other. As we separated, our foreheads still touched for a moment. Then we looked at each other as we walked out of the gate.

We walked on different paths carrying the same memories.

Epilogue

Avinash's Letter

Hey Blunder Queen,

I still remember that I wrote you a letter every year till we turned 8, but then it started to feel childish. Moreover, I was never good with words, but today, I have a lot to say to you.

First, I am proud of you for the way you stood up for mom. When you admitted that you were the one who hit dad, I loved you even more, as if that was even possible. Yes, I was pissed off initially when I saw the police, but on second thought, what you did needed courage. Courage that I didn't have, nor did mom. So, hats off to you, blunder queen. This time your blunder was worth appreciating.

Second, no matter how much we fight, you know I love you. Right? I really try not to get so protective of you. I want to give you space, but I am always scared something or someone might hurt you. I can't help it. You won't understand it because you are not a brother.

Third, I believe no one can love you like your stupid brother, not even that cripple of yours. Ok, sorry, stop sulking at that word. But you know what? I appreciate your choice. This Raksha Bandhan, I am gifting you my support for your cripple, even though the gift is belated. Don't get angry, it's my pet name for him, just like it's Blunder Queen for you. He is a gem of a person and I am happy for you. I am giving this to you in writing so that you can treasure this as the best gift I ever gave you. At least it's better than those ridiculously pink things!

Now, just because I wrote you a letter this year doesn't mean you can expect a letter from me every year. This is my last letter. Got it?

And mind you, no matter how much we fight or how much you try to avoid me, after every fight, I am going to return to you to freak you out.

-Your stupid loving brother.

Kangana

'I need a rebirth to feel love again.'

That's what Vivaan said when he proposed to me. Wasn't it strange? He said he liked me a lot, a lot, but he wasn't sure if he loved me. He was honest, and instead of pushing me away, his honesty made me fall harder for him.

"We can survive on the love I feel." I had said, and we started our new journey.

Sometime back he made a painting of me and his mother and said it was his favourite painting. And as he said that, I knew he could make an exact replica with two different people, his first love and his first mother. And I was fine with it.

Once he painted something strange - his canvas was filled with random strokes, just messing up the space. I asked him what it was. He smiled when he looked at me. He knew I didn't understand art much. I hope he knew that I still understood the artist perfectly. "It's love, only love can be that complicated." He had replied.

Yes, love was complicated. And that's why I couldn't decide what I felt as he held our daughter for the first time, lifted her in the air, and cried, "I am reborn,"

Dev

I believe that humans, like computers, have different versions that are updated sometimes by situations, sometimes by scars. I never met the first version of Avni, though I always wanted to know what she was like. The version I saw of her was broken and fragile. She had lost her brother and her love. She never told me about her love, though she did offer to tell me about her past. But I didn't want to know. I too had a past, but I never loved the way Avni did. There were nights she cried in her sleep, calling out his name 'Vivaan' with a longing so deep that it broke me. I hugged her and she held on to me, maybe thinking I was someone else. But I never hated her for that. What happened was before I entered her life, and if this was the depth of her love, I thought I might be lucky enough to be a part of her heart again. And yes, her heart was mended and she gave it to me. It was still fragile but I promised to protect it. And then she never called his name in her sleep. But what did I do? Shattered it into a thousand pieces. I lost everything when I lost her.

She was always kind to Tia, but I wanted more than a façade for our family. I wanted our family to be bound by love and not duty. And to tell the truth, I had lost all hope. But Avni was a different person since she returned from India two years ago. When she hugged me at the airport, I was taken aback. Tia also returned a happier person; their bonding had gone to a different level. They just couldn't stop hugging and kissing each other. Tia even complained that Avni was suffocating her by hugging her so hard. When Tia said she went to some nice uncle's home whose name was Vivaan, my eyes met with Avni's but she didn't say anything and I didn't ask. I liked this new version of

Avni, no matter what the reason was. And Avni again started screaming the name of the person she had lost in her sleep, but this time the name was 'Dev'. I never needed any other proof that life had given me a second chance. Step by step we rebuilt a new world, a happier place. The past was still there—sometimes I could see it in her eyes and she can could witness it in mine—but with all the cracks, we are happy in this new version of our life. And happy could have different meanings for different people.

"Mumma, I want a sister." Tia said, "Ugh, Mumma leave me, you have hugged me too tight". Avni kissed her on the cheek. "I already have a princess. Now I want a prince." She touched her womb. She was seven months pregnant.

"Have you thought of a name?" Tia asked.

"Yes," she smiled with tears. "Avinash."

Vedika

It was about midnight. I tiptoed to my laptop after my husband and Munna slept. It had been long since she wrote to me. Anxiety flowed through me as I opened my mailbox, but seeing her name flash in my inbox suddenly lifted my mood.

Dear Vedika,

The way I was getting impatient to write to you, I still can't believe I once hated you. The long days with nothing much to do in the hospital reminded me of the hurricane of emotions I had experienced when I found your letter in Vivaan's closet. Everything changed that day. The pain dripping from your words strangely connected me to you. I don't know how you must feel because my story was entirely different from yours, but I have known pain too. Well, in retrospect, who hasn't?

Well, this is not the time to talk about pain. I want to share some good news. Do you know why I was in the hospital? My daughter-in-law was advised bed-rest in her last trimester, but now, after the delivery, she is perfectly fine. The baby has arrived. Congratulations to both of us. We are now grandmothers! Sending you the photo of the little one in the attached file.

Once again, as in every email, I want you to know that if you ever want to connect to Vivaan, he is just a phone call away. Until then, I will keep you two connected through our secret conversations.

Keep smiling.

-Nidhi

I opened the photo with trembling hands. It was the prettiest sight of my life. My little granddaughter was sleeping peacefully in her daddy's arms. For the first time in years, I cried incessantly out of joy.

Sometimes, we grow bit by bit but sometimes, we grow up in a moment. A moment that's ruthless, a robber that steals a part of us. A moment that becomes a secret companion for life. But with time we learn to smile, sometimes even at the memories we once cried at, and that smile doesn't mean that the scars have healed. It just means that we have learned to live with the scars, that we are ready for the joys we long ignored, and that finally, we have accepted the life beyond scars.

The End.

Next Book In The Series

**Beyond Lies – A nail biting psychological thriller
with a killer twist.**

ALKA DIMRI SAKLANI
BEYOND
SOME SINS CAN'T BE FORGIVEN
LIES

Hi, I am Tia Bakshi. Nobody knows where I am. Hell, even I don't know where I am. I don't even know who my captor is, my blindfold doesn't allow me to see anything. I don't even know how this will end. Can anyone be more clueless about their lives?

Tied up in this jilted place I have little to do, but reminiscence my old life. I had it all; a loving family, a dependable friend, a compassionate fiancé, a dream job. I never had time to analyze my relationships then, but now in this god-forsaken place, amid fear and doubts, all I have is time and I can see the cracks I ignored for so long. And I am forced to question; was my life really perfect? Or was it a perfect lie?

Twisted and dark, Beyond Lies, explores the complexities of the human mind, a mind that can lead to dangerous paths and sometimes, harm the one it seeks to protect.

Acknowledgment And A Note To Readers

I take this opportunity to thank everyone who has been a part of my writing journey and motivated me in different ways.

First and foremost, I am thankful to you, my dear reader, for picking up this book and reading the words that I write. I am grateful for all the love and support you have shown me over the years.

I would also like to express my gratitude to Asha Dimri and Animesh Nautiyal for beta reading my book and having the patience to read many versions of the same write-up.

A special thanks to my author friends for all the support they send my way; from helping me finalize the cover design to helping me attain a higher word count on a daily basis, I can always count on them. Thanks to my family and friends, who motivate me in ways I can't even describe in words. I would also like to thank my husband, Gaurav Saklani, and my kids Arnav and Aryan, for being patient with me when I spend more time with my characters than I do with them.

A special thanks to Notion Press, for showing trust in my work and helping me to reach a wider audience.

Finally, thank you God for this book and everything.

If you want to stay updated about my next release follow me on my Facebook page.

https://www.facebook.com/Alkadimrisaklani/

Or follow me on Instagram

https://www.instagram.com/alka_saklani/

See you again on the pages on my other stories, which are listed below.

Mystery/Thriller
<u>45 Days in a Cancer Hospital</u>
<u>Beyond Lies</u>

Contemporary Fiction/Romance
<u>Beyond Secrets</u>
<u>Beyond Scars</u>
<u>The Autumn of Love</u>
<u>Against Time & Destiny</u>

Short Stories
<u>A Promise that Changed Everything</u>
<u>20 Year School Reunion</u>
Take care and stay safe.
Love,
Alka